NIGHT OF THE LIVING TREKKIES

BY KEVIN DAVID ANDERSON
AND SAM STALL

QUIRK BOOKS
PHILADELPHIA

And

Library of Congress Cataloging in Publication Number: 2010928603

ISBN: 978-1-59474-463-1

Printed in Canada

Typeset in Bembo, House 3009, and OCRA

Designed by Doogie Horner
Production management by John J. McGurk
Cover illustration by Glen Orbik

Distributed in North America by Chronicle Books
680 Second Street
San Francisco, CA 94107

10 9 8 7 6 5 4 3 2 1

Quirk Books
215 Church Street
Philadelphia, PA 19106
www.irreference.com
www.quirkbooks.com

ATTENTION ALL STARFLEET PERSONNEL

The following text is an original work
of fiction/horror/parody. <u>Night of the
Living Trekkies</u> is not sponsored by,
affiliated with, or endorsed by the
owners of the <u>Star Trek</u>® brand. Any
personnel claiming otherwise will be
sentenced to one year of hard labor in
the penal colony of Rura Penthe.

"It isn't all over; everything has not been invented;
the human adventure is just beginning."
—Gene Roddenberry

"Horror is the genre that never dies."
—George A. Romero

space seed

"Space, the final frontier . . . "

"Shut up."

"These are the voyages of the starship *Enterprise* . . . "

"I said, shut up."

"Its five-year mission: to explore strange worlds, to seek out new life and new civilizations . . . "

"You're pissing me off."

"To boldly go where no man has gone before."

"Quit rubbing it in, okay?"

First Lieutenant Mallory Kaplan, U.S. Air Force Medical Service flight nurse, finished her recital and smiled triumphantly.

"Actually, that last bit doesn't quite capture the current situation," she said. "Plenty of men—and women—have already gone where I'm going. But I'll be the first person *currently in this room* to make the trip."

The room of which she spoke was an underground bunker. She and her senior watch officer, U.S. Air Force Captain Les Marple, spent four eight-hour shifts inside it each week, studying images and readouts on computer monitors. During the long, boring stretches when nothing inside the almost completely automated facility required their attention, they passed the time by harassing each other.

"You're being unprofessional," Marple said. "I'm your superior officer. Show some respect."

"Can't help it," Kaplan said. "I'm so excited about my uniform."

"You're dressing up?"

"Of course. That's half the fun of attending a Star Trek convention. I'm portraying one of the greatest captains ever to command the *Enterprise*."

"You mean Kirk?"

"Kirk's a man."

"I know, but I think you could pull it off."

Kaplan smacked him lightly on the head with her clipboard.

"I'm going as Captain Rachel Garrett," she said.

Marple shot Kaplan a puzzled look.

"Who the hell is that?" he said.

"The captain of the *Enterprise*-C, which served a couple of decades before the *Enterprise*-D from *Star Trek: The Next Generation*. A temporal rift brought it forward in time, changing future history. In order to repair the damage, it had to go back to its own era, even though . . . "

"Yeah, yeah, yeah," Marple said. "Seen it, bought the Blu-ray. What's the point of going as someone so obscure? No one will recognize you."

Kaplan's sly smile let him know that he'd walked into a trap.

"Oh, that's right," she said with mock concern. "You've never *been* to GulfCon. You don't know that the convention attendees like to go as incredibly obscure Trek characters. It's a joke that started at the first one, five years ago. If you make it through the entire weekend without anyone guessing your identity, you win a hundred bucks."

"Screw that," Marple said. "I'd go as Picard. He's what inspired me to join the Air Force. I kept thinking that one day I'd be exploring space and commanding my own ship."

"Me, too," Kaplan said wistfully. "How's that working out for you?"

Marple surveyed his surroundings. The bunker in which the two of them sat was located on the grounds of the Johnson Space-flight Center, just outside Houston, Texas. Not that the general public—or, for that matter, most of the center's staff—knew that. Their duty station, secured behind a steel door that opened only to those who passed a retinal scan, was a dimly lit, concrete-floored room with a single long desk, upon which sat two massive computer monitors—monitors that formed the centers of their professional lives.

"Not exactly like I'd hoped," Marple said.

"At least you're bald, like Picard," Kaplan said.

"I'd rather have no hair than Janeway hair. *First season* Janeway hair."

"You'd also make a great Orion. Since you're already green with envy."

Marple was about to tell Kaplan to stick her high-horse attitude straight up her Jefferies tube when a single *ding* emanated from the monitors parked in front of them.

"Box Seventeen," Kaplan said, suddenly all business.

Marple's fingers flew across his keyboard. A grainy black-and-white shot of a steel-walled enclosure popped up on both their screens. Inside, a small four-legged animal paced back and forth twice. Then, with its head pointed squarely into a corner, it stopped.

"Haven't seen this one before," Kaplan said. "It looks like it's been partially skinned."

"Back in the day, when they were still working on these things, some genius decided to vivisect it," Marple said. "Or maybe *dissect* is the correct word. It didn't go according to plan. The guy who tried it is in Box Thirty-two."

Kaplan dutifully noted the incident in her log. Not that it was necessary. Everything—absolutely *everything*—that happened in the facility was closely monitored at an off-site command center. There was no need to send reports. The Brass watched it all in real time.

"We're getting dinged a lot today," she said. "It's like they're restless or something."

Marple laughed.

"They're not restless," he said. "They're not anything. They go in one direction until they hit a wall, then go in another until they hit another wall."

"Still," Kaplan said, "four dings is a lot."

Marple knew she was right. Often entire shifts passed without movement. The four incidents they'd logged so far were noteworthy. Especially since they'd all occurred in the last two hours. Each came from a different specimen, two of which had gone months without so much as a twitch. Yet today they got up and walked. Or staggered. Or crawled.

It was unprecedented. Kaplan and Marple hated it when the unprecedented happened, because there was always the chance that it could quickly morph into something horrible. Something that could never, ever be allowed to see the light of day. Like the guy in Box Thirty-two.

"Sometimes I wish I was still back in a silo, serving on a Minuteman missile crew," Marple said. "It was less stressful."

"Isn't that why they picked you for this?" Kaplan said.

"Yeah. My psych profile was exactly what they wanted. Someone who wouldn't mind spending a lot of time underground staring at the end of the world."

His monitor emitted a muted alarm.

"What?" Kaplan said. "What is it?"

Marple studied the readouts on his screen. His eyes grew wide.

"There's a problem with the security system," he said. "Big-time malfunction."

"What kind?" Kaplan said.

Marple looked at the screen for a few seconds more.

"We've lost containment on boxes Nine and Twelve."

"Does that mean . . . ?"

"Give me a visual on Twelve," Marple said. "Maybe it's a false reading."

Another black-and-white image of a steel-lined cell appeared on their monitors. It was empty.

"Switch to exterior," Marple said.

The view showed Twelve's door. A door that hadn't been un-sealed, so far as they knew, in more than two years.

Now it was wide open.

"We're screwed," Kaplan said. "We're totally screwed."

"Keep it together," Marple said, sweat beads dotting his forehead as he typed. "A computer glitch sprung them. But we're safe in here. Nothing can get through a two-inch steel door."

"Dammit," Kaplan said. "More of them are opening! Lost con-tainment on Thirty, Twenty-Five, Eight . . . "

"Stop. I get it. Check Box One."

Kaplan switched to the enclosure just in time for them to see the door open, revealing a rectangle of impenetrable blackness.

The two watched the doorway in terrified fascination. The room's interior camera had malfunctioned months earlier. Since no one was allowed into the room under any circumstances, the creature lurking in Box One remained a mystery.

"Maybe it's dead," Kaplan whispered as they both watched their screens. "I mean, *really* dead."

Almost before she got the words out, something shambled out of the darkness. The thing was naked, but it was impossible to tell its sex. Its desiccated skin was drawn tightly over its skeleton. Its hair was gone, its eyes had shrunk into their sockets, and its lips were drawn back over its teeth in a permanent grin.

Yet it walked.

"That's twenty feet down the hall," Kaplan said. "We've got to get out of here."

"No," Marple said. "Something's opening every computer-controlled door in the place. We step out there and we're dead. Worse than dead."

"*Every* computer-controlled door?" she asked.

Marple caught her meaning. They turned together and gazed at the back of the room. Just in time to see the door to their duty station glide open.

Outside in the darkness, something moaned.

Kaplan reached out and grabbed Marple's hand.

"I'm sorry I said you were bald," she whispered.

"I'm sorry I said you had Janeway hair," he replied.

Marple looked up at the ceiling-mounted video camera perched directly in front of them, dispassionately transmitting everything to the off-site command center.

"What are you waiting for?" he shouted at it. "For God's sake, just do it!"

Five hundred miles away, a two-star general leaned over the shoulder of a technician, watching the nurse and the former missile commander's last moments. The general rubbed the back of his neck, surveyed the frightened faces of the half-dozen officers surrounding him, and then spoke.

"That's it," he said. "Detonate the fail-safe weapon. Deploy the cover story."

1

A Private Little War

It was late winter of 2009 and Jim Pike was in Afghanistan.

He'd arrived there a few weeks earlier with the rest of his U.S. Army unit, the 10th Mountain Division's 3rd Brigade Combat Team. It was windy and cold, and the mountainous terrain looked like another world. A world composed almost entirely of steep slopes and thousand-foot drops.

He was twenty-three years old and in full battle dress, leading a squad of soldiers through an outlying neighborhood of Asadabad, the capital of Kunar province. Kunar was a flyspeck of land wedged hard against the Pakistani border. In good times it sheltered smugglers moving everything from illegally harvested lumber to drugs. In bad times—and these were very, very bad times—it harbored guerillas of every stripe, from al Qaeda to the Taliban to mujahideen.

Asadabad, a maze of narrow streets and walled compounds sheltering roughly half the province's thirty thousand people, was their unofficial capital. The troops called it A-Bad.

Jim watched his six-member squad, the lead element in a three-platoon-strong raiding party supported by Stryker combat vehicles and Apache helicopter gunships, move down a dusty, crooked street.

They kept an eye out for snipers and covered one another as they advanced. An old man sitting on the curb, his ragged, mud-colored *chapan* pulled tight against the cold, barely acknowledged their passing.

They stopped near the door of a weather-worn house. They were pretty sure, based on drone images presented during the pre-raid briefing, that it harbored a cache of contraband weapons. The boxes stacked in the building's dusty courtyard, plainly visible in the photos, were the right shape and size.

The soldier on point tried the door. It was locked.

Jim was about to order an entry. Then, out of the corner of his eye, he saw the old man in the chapan stand up and disappear down an alley. In Afghanistan it was never a good sign when people vanished like that. It meant they knew something was about to happen. And that they didn't want to be around when it did.

"Hold up," Jim said.

But his soldiers didn't seem to hear. They bunched up at the entrance, ready to begin.

"Hold up!" Jim yelled.

No one listened. One soldier kicked down the door and charged into the blackness. Two more followed.

An explosion rocked the street. Dust and flames poured out of the doorway. The concussion blew one of the soldiers out of the house. He lay on the ground, clutching his face.

The other two didn't come out at all.

Jim rushed into the burning building, trying to locate the missing soldiers in the choking blackness. He staggered around for what felt like forever, walked for what seemed like miles. Slowly, it dawned on him that he couldn't possibly still be in that tiny, bombed-out dwelling on the fringe of A-Bad.

That's when he found his soldiers.

The missing were privates Eric Willman and Lou Jones. Both were new to the 3rd. Both were covered with blood, their uniforms shredded and blackened. Yet both were on their feet, standing calmly at parade rest.

"Why didn't you listen to me?" Jim asked.

"We couldn't," Lou said. "You weren't here."

The two, Jim realized, were dead. Yet there they stood, giving him looks that could have burned holes in stone.

"We were your responsibility," Eric said.

"Where were you?" they both asked.

Jim tried to answer, but no words came out.

"Where were you?" they asked once more.

Again, Jim struggled to speak.

"Wake up," someone else said.

The darkness lightened, the faces of the dead soldiers faded. A new, only slightly less insistent voice replaced theirs.

"Wake up!" it shouted. "Some kid's going nuts with a phaser."

Jim sat up. The newspaper draped over his lap fell to the floor. He rubbed his forehead and looked around. Afghanistan was gone. So was 2009. Instead, he found himself sitting in a heavily upholstered chair in the lobby of the Botany Bay Hotel and Conference Center in downtown Houston. It was late afternoon on a Friday.

And he was asleep on the job.

The owner of the voice stood over him, a disapproving scowl drawing tight lines across her sun-worn face.

"Hey, Janice," he grunted. "How's it going?"

"You're lucky the GM likes you," replied Janice Bohica, placing her hands on the sides of her head as if to steady a throbbing brain. "But why, I have no idea. You're the last person in the world I'd trust with responsibility."

Jim had heard this spiel before. He suspected that Janice honed it on a long string of underlings during her oft-referenced seventeen years as the hotel's daytime manager.

"What can I do for you?" he asked.

"How about getting your act together and behaving like a grown-up? In case you haven't noticed, we're shorthanded today."

Jim glanced around the lobby, which was uncharacteristically quiet for a Friday afternoon. "Looks like everything's under control," he said. "Aside from two or three hundred Trekkies, we're pretty much empty."

"We have precisely 262 registered GulfCon guests," Janice said, "but we'll have north of three thousand walk-ins for the convention. These people can be very high maintenance. You're going to be running all weekend."

Jim sat up in the chair and yawned.

"What were you saying about a guy with a Taser?"

"Phaser," Janice corrected. "One of those handheld ray guns from *Star Trek*. There's a kid on the second floor and he's pointing it at guests. Scaring people."

"Where's our chief of security?"

"Dexter's busy. Someone from the seventh floor reported a drunk mime. The guy actually attacked someone."

"A drunk *mime*?" Jim said.

"A man in a leotard with his face painted. Tried to jump Dexter, too. But Dexter laid him out with his baton, cuffed him, and brought him down for the cops."

"Crap," Jim said. "He'll be filling out forms for hours."

"Exactly," Janice said. "Which is why you're dealing with phaser boy."

"You can count on me."

"I've heard that before," Janice said. "But I know you don't mean it. Your goal in life is to *avoid* being counted on."

Jim felt his discomfort level rising. Janice was bitchy. She was officious. But the thing that irritated him the most was that she totally had him pegged.

"Look, enough of the psychotherapy, all right?" he asked. "I get it; I'm a drag on your existence. Why do you want to spend more of it cataloging my shortcomings?"

Janice looked him up and down.

"Because you could be more than this," she said, gesturing at his hotel uniform. "It really doesn't become you."

Jim felt a keen desire to change the subject, so he knelt and gathered up his newspaper—that morning's edition of the *Houston Chronicle*. He surveyed the front-page headline before placing it neatly on the chair's side table: JOHNSON SPACEFLIGHT CENTER LOCKED DOWN.

"A gas leak caused an explosion," Janice explained. "It's been cordoned off for the recovery crews. They're going over the whole place with tweezers."

"Sounds like you're following the story pretty closely."

"Current events are important, Jim. Especially current events happening fifteen miles away. Now, please go fetch that phaser kid."

Janice turned abruptly and walked back toward the front desk.

Jim stood up and ran his hands through his close-cropped chestnut hair. He kept it only slightly longer than the buzz cut he'd worn in the army. But his hotel uniform was radically different. Instead of desert camouflage, a helmet, and body armor, he wore black boots, black khakis, and a white mock turtleneck under a red double-breasted jacket. It wasn't exactly the best choice for Houston in August, but inside the hermetically sealed Botany Bay, where the hyperactive climate-control system chilled everything to a crisp sixty-eight degrees, it was tolerable.

Certainly, it was more tolerable than the place he'd just come from.

He walked quickly through the hotel's sunlit seventeen-story atrium. The side and rear walls were lined with hotel room windows. The north-facing wall held the main entrance—a battery of glass doors. Across from it was the front desk—a long, black marble check-in counter.

Just past the front desk sat a bank of four glass-enclosed elevators. Jim pressed the call button and then fished a walkie-talkie from his jacket's interior vest pocket. Someone had written "Property of BBH&CC" on its back with a Sharpie.

"Hey, Dexter, are you there?" he said.

"I'm in my office," came the reply. "Administering first aid."

"To who?"

"To myself. That clowny son of a bitch sank his teeth into my arm."

"You're serious? You were bitten by a mime?"

"It's not funny, Pike. I'm bleeding. I just poured a gallon of hydrogen peroxide on this thing."

Jim was tempted to reply that he'd seen worse wounds in his lifetime, but there was no point in trying to explain it to a civilian. "I'm going to pick up this phaser kid," he said. "You want me to bring him down to your office?"

"Hell, no, just bring me his toy," Dexter said. "I don't want to call the cops again. It took forever for them to pick up Marcel Marceau."

The elevator on the far right of the bank dinged. Its doors opened and Jim stepped inside. "I'm on my way," he said as the doors closed. "See you in a few minutes."

Jim slid the walkie-talkie into his jacket, stepped aboard the elevator, and pushed the button for the second floor. Playing on the hotel audio system was a scratchy recording of William Shatner singing "Lucy in the Sky with Diamonds." The GulfCon organizers had prepared an entire playlist that was tailored exclusively to Trekkie conventioneers; there were pop songs covered by Leonard Nimoy, film scores by Jerry Goldsmith, and the occasional warbling song of a humpback whale. Jim guessed this last bit was a nod to *Star Trek IV: The Voyage Home*, but really it was anybody's guess.

A moment later, the elevator doors opened, revealing a wild-eyed teen wearing a T-shirt that read "There Can Be Only One Kirk." He pointed a plastic phaser at Jim and squeezed the trigger. The toy emitted a blast of bright red light.

"Toh-pah!" the kid shouted.

Jim's hand darted out and grabbed Mr. Phaser by the wrist— then yanked him into the elevator and pressed him up against the wall. The move was all reflex. He didn't even need to think about it.

"You shouldn't point guns at people," he said. "The last person who did that to me ended up in a rubber bag."

The teen, thoroughly terrorized, dropped his toy.

Jim reached down to pick it up, ashamed of himself for over-reacting. It's not like this high school sophomore was a threat to anyone. He just needed a little discipline.

"Look, why don't you just go to your room?" Jim suggested. "Go watch TV or something."

"TV's busted."

Wonderful, Jim thought. *Another problem*.

He asked the kid for his room number and then tried to clarify the issue. "You mean the TV's broken? Or you're not getting a clear picture?"

"It's static," the kid explained.

Jim promised to send up a maintenance person by the end of the day. "And you can get your toy back after the convention. Ask for it when you check out."

He was back in the lobby a minute later and emerged from the elevator to find a pretty, young woman waiting for the lift. Judging from her navy-blue suit and Coach handbag, he guessed she'd arrived on business.

The woman smiled at him. "Nice costume."

Jim looked down at his red hotel jacket—and the toy phaser—and realized she had mistaken him for a Trekkie. "I'm not here for the convention," he sheepishly explained. "I work with the hotel."

She stepped aboard the elevator. "Then you might want to holster your ray gun."

Jim started to protest further, but it was too late. The doors were already sliding shut.

It's going to be that kind of weekend, he thought.

At the front desk, he passed a member of the maintenance crew who teetered on a ladder, struggling to hang a banner reading "Welcome Fifth Annual GulfCon" over the check-in area. Jim stepped behind the counter and through a doorway, walking past banks of cubicles until he reached an actual office with regular walls. The sign on its closed door read "Chief of Security." Jim used the butt of the phaser to knock.

"Enter," came a voice from the other side.

Jim walked into the office of Dexter Remmick and tossed the toy phaser into a large box of lost-and-found objects. Dexter's more than three-hundred-pound bulk was wedged behind his metal desk, whose surface was strewn with the contents of the hotel's first-aid kit. A fresh bandage cocooned his left forearm.

"Well, well," Dexter said. "The Assistant Uniformed Staff Manager has decided to bless us with his presence. How was your nap?"

"Very refreshing," Jim said. "Thanks for sending Janice after me."

"My pleasure. How's that promotion treating you?"

Jim smiled grimly as he sat down. He'd spent most of his six months at the Botany Bay as a lowly bellhop. His "promotion"—now a standing joke between Dexter and himself—happened out of the blue. The general manager called him into his office one day and said he'd heard good things about his "management style" and his ability to "energize" the rest of the uniformed staff.

Dexter had guessed, accurately, that much of Jim's vaunted "leadership style" sprang from the fact that he was six foot two and a muscular two hundred and twenty pounds. Which tended to produce excellent compliance when he asked staffers to do things. Like the time he cornered Ted, the pool guy, and warned him to stop leering at female guests while cleaning the filters. Ted seemed thoroughly motivated after that encounter.

"Any more motivated and he would have pissed himself," Dexter had joked at the time.

"When are these people going to realize I took this job to *avoid* responsibility?" Jim said.

"You and me both, buddy," Dexter said. "I'm having zero luck with that today. Kevin should have had my back when I collected that goddamned mime, but he's home sick. Right now, I'm the only law west of the Pecos."

"At least we're not full up," Jim offered.

"Thank God for that. If this place was hopping, we'd be screwed. People have been calling in sick all day."

He scowled at his bandage. The gauze was starting to turn pink.

"You need to get that looked at," Jim said. "It's bleeding way too much."

"I'll take care of it after work," Dexter said. "Things are too hectic for me to duck out of here."

"Hectic, huh? Then I better switch to Emergency Mode."

"What's that?

Jim stood up to leave. "It's where I toss my walkie-talkie down the fire stairwell and hide in the freight elevator."

"Sounds like a plan. And say hello to Sarah for me."

"What are you talking about?" Jim said.

"You think I'm stupid? Every time you visit me, you find an excuse to visit the new girl's cubicle. It must be instinctive. Like those sparrows that fly back to Caracas every year."

"It's swallows, and they fly back to Capistrano," Jim said. "But I get your point. I'll tell her you said hi."

"And watch your back," Dexter added. "That mime could have friends."

"I really doubt that mimes have friends," Jim said as he walked out the door.

He found Sarah Cornell, the hotel's recently hired twenty-five-year-old assistant catering coordinator, sitting in her cubicle.

"Hey," he said. "How's the food business?"

Sarah glanced up from her desk. She looked tired.

"I need thirty pounds of edible jelly worms for one of the Gulf-Con banquets. They'll be part of an alien buffet—something called goog."

"You mean *gagh*," Jim corrected. "It's a type of worm favored by Klingons."

"Whatever, nerd," Sarah said. "I'm driving to a warehouse club to buy some."

"It's gotta be a hundred and ten degrees outside."

"Doesn't matter. Neither rain nor snow nor extreme heat shall stay this courier from getting a bunch of fake worms for sci-fi geeks to nosh on. And then I'm sneaking home early. I really, really need to take off my bra."

"I can help with that," Jim offered. "I'm kind of an expert."

"No, seriously. Look at this."

Sarah pulled back her blue silk blouse to reveal her bare right shoulder. Just below her collarbone sat a purplish bruise about the size of a lemon. Her bra overlapped its edge.

"Itches like crazy," she said.

"You should see a doctor," Jim said.

"If I had health insurance, I would. But our company has a three-month probationary period for new hires." Sarah retrieved her purse from under her desk and stood up. "Can you do me a favor?"

"Of course."

"Rodriguez is setting up a dinner buffet in the exposition hall. We're waiting on a big cake shaped like a . . . a . . . "

She retrieved a sticky note from beside her computer.

"A D7-class Klingon battle cruiser. But I can't get anyone at the bakery to take my call. So, you need to give Rodriguez their phone number, okay?"

Sarah handed him the sticky note, and Jim noticed a wad of tissue wrapped around her right index finger.

"My neighbor's four-year-old bit me," she explained.

"You're serious?" he asked. "Dexter was just telling me he—"

"I couldn't believe it," Sarah continued. "Little brat sneaked up on me while I was walking to my car. I thought he was going to chomp it right off."

She showed him the wound—just some bloody, baby-tooth-sized dents. But as Jim watched, the dents welled up with blood. Sarah wiped them with the crumpled tissue and then threw it in her trash can. A can that was already half full of bloody scraps.

"It's not the end of the world," she assured him. "Just find Rodriguez for me, all right?"

Sarah stepped out of her cubicle and walked away. Jim watched her leave.

Then he looked down at the note. It was speckled with bright red flecks of fresh blood.

CHAPTER

2

Balance of Terror

Little kids bite grown-ups every day, Jim told himself. And a drunk mime nipping a security guard was nothing to get worked up about. It was just a weird coincidence.

Yet his famed "spider sense" was tingling.

Jim had learned to trust his instincts during his first combat tour, when he realized he always seemed to know, maybe half a minute before everyone else, that the crap was going to hit the fan. His sergeant said it reminded him of how dogs can tell when an earthquake is coming.

He earned his reputation early in that first deployment. He was on patrol with his unit, marching down a rutted gash in the ground that the locals generously called a road. Beside it sat an old, rusted-out pickup truck that looked like it had been there since before the Soviets invaded. Jim's unit had marched past it a dozen times on a dozen different days. The wreck was part of the landscape.

Except this time. As they approached it, Jim sensed something awry. He couldn't put his finger on exactly what, but he felt it so strongly that he summoned the nerve to mention it to the captain leading the patrol. Not surprisingly, the captain ordered him to elaborate.

"The vegetation around the truck—it's been disturbed," Jim said, thinking fast. "I think someone's been screwing around over there."

Which, Jim figured, *might* have been true. Perhaps that's the particular detail his ever-alert subconscious registered. What mattered was that his unit gave the truck a wide berth. And that later the captain notified ordnance disposal, which opened its hood and found two freshly placed 105-millimeter artillery shells linked to a radio-controlled detonator. Whoever was supposed to press the button was long gone.

So, he knew he had a sixth sense about danger. It served him well in combat zones, where he understood the threats. But now he was standing in the middle of a two-star hotel on a sunny August day, surrounded by innocent civilians, while his internal shit-storm detector buzzed for attention. He didn't have a clue what it wanted.

Maybe I'm just bored, Jim thought. *Maybe I'm so tired of this bellhop crap that my unconscious is trying to manufacture something for me to worry about.*

He held Sarah's note between his thumb and index finger as he walked the long, long hallway linking the lobby to the Endeavour Room, its main exhibition hall. To his right, restrooms and storage areas lined the wall. To his left were doors leading to smaller meeting and dining areas. Most had easels out front stating that, at some particular time on Saturday afternoon, they'd host events with names like "Cheating Death Via Transporter" or "Klingons and Bynars and Gorn, Oh My!"

Jim stopped just long enough to read a large poster taped to the door of the auditorium. It explained that Saturday night's keynote address would be given by a Harvard professor named Eli Sandoval, an acclaimed exobiologist and one of the world's leading authorities on the possibilities of extraterrestrial life. Jim wondered how the GulfCon organizers lured a fanboy with Ivy League credentials all the way down to Houston in the middle of August.

By the time he reached the Endeavour Room's entrance, across from the GulfCon registration desk, the blood on Sarah's note had started to dry. It was five fifteen and he was supposed to meet his sister in less than an hour. She and her friends were driving more than a hundred miles to attend the convention and hoped to arrive at six o'clock, or thereabouts.

Jim took out his cell phone and scrolled down the menu to "Rayna."

His sister's cell rang four times before she picked up.

"Hey, Jim," was all he heard before a blast of static overwhelmed the connection.

"Rayna?" he said.

" . . . stupid phone . . . "

"Is everything okay?" Jim asked.

For a moment the static abated.

"We're good," Rayna said. "Traffic's a bear."

"What's wrong with your cell?" Jim said.

" . . . phone connections get worse the closer we get to you . . . "
More static.

"I'm not sure this convention is worth all the effort," Jim said. "You guys might want to detour and hit the beach instead."

His half-shouted message got through. The reply came in fragments.

" . . . really looking forward . . . "

" . . . biggest all-Trek con in the South . . . "

From the background Jim heard a male voice. It said something about nonrefundable room deposits.

"All right," Jim shouted again. "I'll see you soon. But please be careful. And let me know when you're close by, so I can meet you. What are you driving?"

Jim thought he heard laughter.

"You'll see," Rayna said. "And you won't believe your . . . "

Her final words were swallowed by a howl of interference.

Jim looked at the phone, swore under his breath, then snapped it shut and slipped it into his pants pocket. Only then did he notice that his bellowing had drawn the attention of pretty much everyone at the GulfCon registration table.

"Trouble with your communicator?" asked a short, stout man dressed as a Ferengi.

"Subspace interference," Jim said to the fifteen or so Trekkies staring at him. "It's always really bad in this sector."

A Tellerite and a Romulan nodded knowingly.

Rayna's twenty years old, Jim thought. *She's a grown-up. I'm acting like an overprotective father.*

But Jim knew he couldn't help it. He'd played that role ever since their real father had died in an oil refinery accident. Even now, Jim's mental picture of his sister was the indelible image of a ten-year-old girl with tears in her eyes, struggling to understand that Dad wasn't coming home and that from now on she'd have to make do with just a mom and a brother.

Actually, she wasn't even that lucky. Their mother, a borderline alcoholic before the accident, decided to go all the way afterward. She wasn't violent or loud. She just wasn't . . . anything. Every day, Jim would come home from football practice—with Rayna tagging along because after school she didn't have anything else to do but sit in the bleachers and do her homework. And there Mom would be, parked on the couch, sipping wine and watching Springer.

She died from a heart attack while Jim was in Afghanistan. It was yet another example, he told himself, of how he was never around when people really needed him. His little sister picked the casket, planned the funeral, and even spoke at the sparsely attended memorial service.

Jim was discharged from the army two months later. Everything about his relationship with his sister changed. Rayna became the responsible one while he devolved into a lost, frightened child. She was a college junior, powering toward a psychology degree. She had a life. She had friends—even if some of them *were* science-fiction nerds. She had a future.

Meanwhile, Jim was a glorified bellhop. His only "goal" was never again to put himself in a position where others depended on him. Because he knew he'd fail. Just like he failed Rayna. Just like he failed in Afghanistan.

"Excuse me," a voice said, interrupting his reverie. "Are you with the hotel?"

Jim snapped out of his funk. Standing before him was a trim, balding, middle-aged man wearing an impeccably tailored *Voyager*-style medical uniform. He bore an uncanny resemblance to the show's holographic doctor. But Jim instantly recognized him as GulfCon's keynote speaker, the exobiologist from Harvard University.

"How can I help you, Dr. Sandoval?"

The doctor stiffened. "You know who I am?"

"I just saw a poster for your lecture," Jim explained. "It's pretty heroic of you to come all this way just to brief a bunch of Trekkies."

"Oh, it's no trouble at all," Sandoval said, seemingly relieved. "Public outreach is an important part of my job. And I wouldn't miss GulfCon for the world."

"You've been here before?" Jim was a little surprised. There were certainly bigger Trek conventions than GulfCon, and going to Houston in August could hardly be a draw.

"I come every year," Sandoval said. "It's a great place to disseminate . . . news about my work."

"Any big breakthroughs in exobiology?" Jim asked.

"One could say that," Sandoval agreed, smiling. "But you'll have
to wait until tomorrow to learn more. For now, if you could point
me to the men's room, I'd be quite grateful."

Jim pointed the doctor down the hall, then proceeded to the
Endeavour Room. He was confronted by what looked like a vast
outer-space flea market. The front quarter of the expo hall was given
over to vendors. It was lined with rows of eight-feet-wide by twelve-
feet-deep stalls separated by fabric partitions. There were roughly a
hundred vendors on hand—a typical industry-convention exhibitor
floor.

What *wasn't* typical was the stuff they offered. As he made his
way deeper into the convention space, Jim saw booths hawking everything from Star Trek bobblehead figures to Spock and Kirk nutcrack-
ers to Starfleet Academy coffee mugs. There were bottles of Pon Farr
Perfume for Women, a USB webcam shaped like the USS *Enterprise*—
even a full-size replica of the ship captain's chair.

Perfect for the nerd who has everything except a life, Jim thought as he
walked past.

A sparse crowd perused the booths, some of which weren't yet
open for business. GulfCon had officially started at noon, but like most
conventions it wouldn't hit its stride until the weekend. The folks who
turned out early were the hardest of the hardcore, the most eager of
the eager. Jim spotted an old-going-on-elderly man dressed as a
Talosian from the first *Star Trek* pilot episode, "The Cage." Then a
stroller-bound toddler decked out like Balok from "The Corbomite
Maneuver."

No matter the outfit, Jim easily identified them all. That is, until he crossed paths with a man wearing a pink jumpsuit and what appeared to be a werewolf mask.

The costume was so absurd that he wondered if its wearer didn't know GulfCon was a Trek-only affair. This guy looked like a character from a weird Japanese video game.

Yet, the more Jim studied the weird ensemble, the more it tickled his memory.

The werewolf noticed Jim staring at him.

"Go ahead," he said. "I dare you to guess."

Suddenly, it clicked.

"You're a Kzinti from *Star Trek: The Animated Series*."

"Damn!" the man exclaimed. "You're the first person to nail it."

"It's a great costume, but it isn't canon," Jim said.

"That's totally debatable. If you think the cartoon show isn't part of the official Star Trek universe, then how do you explain that Kirk's middle name, Tiberius, was first mentioned in the animated episode, 'Bern'?"

Jim felt a surprisingly strong urge to respond. Back in the day, he'd gone round and round in various Internet chat rooms about whether the obscure animated series, which ran on NBC from 1973 to 1974—a decade and a half before he was born—was a full-fledged part of the Trek universe. He even knew that the wolflike Kzinti were portrayed in pink uniforms because that particular episode's director was color-blind and didn't realize how absurd they looked.

In his younger years, he would have spent hours debating the finer points of Trek continuity with a man dressed as a pink werewolf. But that was before he'd enlisted, before Afghanistan, before he'd sampled the real world. A real world that had annihilated his passion for Star Trek like so much antimatter.

"That's a very interesting point," Jim said curtly to the faux Kz-inti. "I hope you enjoy the remainder of your stay."

He was almost clear of the vendor area when one last booth caught his eye. It was full of lethal-looking edged weapons, all of unfamiliar design. Behind a folding table stood a vision of menace—a giant, scowling linebacker of a man in full Klingon makeup, including a massive cranial crest and braided, reddish-black, shoulder-length hair tumbling down over his dark skin. Every inch of his chiseled, roughly six-foot-eight-inch frame was swathed in impeccably tailored leather and metal armor.

Jim walked up to the booth and examined an exotic-looking, extremely heavy dagger. There was a button on the hilt. When he pressed it, two smaller spring-loaded blades popped out of the base.

"That's a d'k tahg," the big Klingon boomed. "The finest workmanship. A warrior such as yourself could slay many a hu'q with it."

Jim looked down at the blade. He could tell from a glance that the edge was dull.

"None of these are sharpened, right?" Jim said.

The Klingon's demeanor subtly changed.

"You're with the hotel?" he asked.

"Yeah."

"Don't worry, nothing in the booth has an edge," he said. "I have a few pieces with live blades, but they're under lock and key in my room."

Jim thanked him for his cooperation. One of the biggest dangers in hosting a science-fiction convention was the presence of live blades on the show floor. Most people brought them with no real intention of hurting anyone; they were simply seeking an additional degree of verisimilitude. But when attendance skyrocketed and the aisles were jammed with guests, those sharpened blades became a real liability.

All it took was one person pushing and shoving his way through the crowd to get a peek at Patrick Stewart, and the result could be a punctured lung.

"This is an outstanding collection," Jim said. "Do you make all of these yourself?"

The Klingon smiled, revealing a mouthful of pointy fake teeth. Or at least Jim assumed they were fake.

"I am Martock, expert weapons maker and second in command of the bird of prey Plank'Nar."

"No, seriously," Jim said. "Speak English."

"I own a metal-fabricating shop in Atlanta," Martock said. "This stuff's like a sideline for me. A really, really profitable sideline. I do *Lord of the Rings*, *Xena*, *Highlander*, you name it. If you see a movie and like a particular piece of hardware, I can make you a copy."

Jim took in the weapons on display. There were daggers of various lengths, all with contorted, nasty-looking blades. There were also several large, crescent-shape contraptions with three leather-lined handles on one side and four sword points and a continuous yard-long edge on the other.

"Nice bat'leths," he said. "Very authentic looking."

"You'll find no finer swords of honor anywhere in the empire."

"Well, I hope you get lots of business. Turnout looks pretty light so far."

"Sometimes it's slow on the first day of a con," Martock said. "And *that* guy's not helping things, either."

He pointed at the expo hall's temporary stage. Martock's booth was in the last row of the vending area, giving him a direct view of the day's entertainment. As the two of them watched, a fat man sporting a jet-black pompadour, a one-piece sequined jumpsuit, and sickly grayish-green facial makeup took the stage.

"Oh, crap," Martock said, unconsciously taking a step back. "He's going on again."

Jim grinned. "I thought Klingons didn't show fear."

"They'd show it if they had to listen to *this* guy. For the third time today."

"Ladies and gentlemen and otherwise, please give it up for *Elvis Borgsley*," someone announced.

"Really?" Jim asked. "They're serious?"

"He's supposed to be Elvis Presley, if Elvis had been assimilated into the Borg Collective," Martock said. "I'd like to assimilate him into the trunk of my car. At least until the end of the con."

Borgsley headed toward the microphone with stunted, mechanical movements. He launched into an off-key ballad called "Are You Isolated from the Collective Tonight?"

"Why do they keep bringing him out?" Jim said.

"It's all they have," Martock replied, visibly pained. "There was supposed to be a Trek metal band called Warp Core Breach, but they're late."

"Bummer," Jim said.

He was about to walk away when he noticed a cot in the back of Martock's booth. Someone was lying on it, but all he could see was a pair of dirty women's athletic shoes sticking out from under a blanket.

"Who's your friend?" he asked, pointing to the cot.

"My business partner, Karen," Martock explained. "She does custom-tailored uniforms—Klingon, Cardassian, all the generations of Starfleet. Really nice work."

"Is she okay?"

"She's just hungover. She went out on the town last night. When she finally crawled back this morning, all she said was that she felt like crap and needed to crash. I hate to think how many commissions she's missing."

"She might have a bug," Jim said. "There's definitely something going around."

"Or maybe she ate off that nasty buffet over there," Martock said, pointing to the room's far corner. "It's been sitting out all day, with no attendants, no nothing."

Jim suddenly remembered Rodriguez and the note in his hand.

"I'll check into it," he said. "Enjoy Mr. Borgsley."

Martock offered a halfhearted wave.

Jim walked to the buffet and found a typical breakfast spread of bagels, sausage, eggs, and cartons of milk and juice. But it wasn't breakfast anymore. Not even close. The drink cartons floated in a tub of lukewarm water that had formerly been ice. The Sterno candle under the warming tray for the sausage had gone out.

Jim glanced around the room for Rodriguez or one of his minions. But there wasn't a single hotel employee in sight. He took out his walkie-talkie.

"Rodriguez," he called. "Are you there?"

No response. Jim stalked through a nearby door, into a service area. He found shelves lined with tablecloths, silverware, warming trays, and napkins, all where they should be. Deeper in the storeroom he passed crates of bottled water, soft drinks, and canned goods—just a small portion of the mountain of foodstuffs the Botany Bay kept on hand at all times, tucked away in various kitchens, freezers, and pantries.

But still no staffers.

Jim walked toward an exterior door where the hotel used to take deliveries. It led outside to an accessway—really just a wide alley— bracketed on one side by the hotel, and on the other by an office building.

He pushed open the heavy steel door and was rewarded with a blast of bright Texas sunshine. The humidity was stifling. He immediately started to sweat.

And almost immediately he spotted Rodriguez, leaning against the wall with a soda bottle in his hand.

"What are you doing out here?" Jim said. "You've got a breakfast buffet that's about to go viral."

"I've been running around all day," Rodriguez countered. "I'm just taking five minutes to catch my breath. And it'd be a lot more relaxing if I wasn't being spied on."

"I'm sorry," Jim said. "Sarah sent me."

"I don't mean you. I mean *them*."

Rodriguez pointed to the far end of the alley, which opened up next to the Botany Bay's front entrance. A trick of architecture cast it into deep shadow. Jim could make out a couple of dumpsters and little else. But the longer he stared, the more convinced he became that there were people in the gloom. Several, actually. And they were looking at him.

"Who are they?" Jim asked.

"Homeless guys. There's always a couple down there. Nice shady spot on a hot day. But for some reason they've been giving me the eye."

"All the more reason to go back to work." Jim handed him the note from Sarah. "She wants you to call this bakery. It's about some kind of . . . "

"D7 battle cruiser cake," Rodriguez said, nodding. "I'll deal with it."

Jim watched Rodriguez step back inside and then held the door for himself. Before returning to the storage room, he glanced one last time at the end of the alley.

The people in the dark were still watching.

It was odd, but it didn't really add up to anything. The bites on Dexter and Sarah were strange, too . . . but so what?

Jim stepped back into the hotel and closed the door behind him.

This isn't Afghanistan, he thought, repeating his personal mantra. *I'm not responsible for any of the trivial bullshit that happens in this stupid hotel. None of it really matters—and amen to that.*

Just then his walkie-talkie chirped for attention. Jim pulled it out and toggled it on.

"Yeah?" he said.

"Your sister just called." The voice belonged to Oscar, the security guard who manned the control booth in the hotel garage. "She'll be here in five minutes. Her friends reserved a spot in our secured parking area."

"Damn it," Jim said.

"You're welcome. You coming?"

"Right away. Where do I go?"

"Space K-7."

"That's a bus slot."

"Which suggests they're arriving in a bus. But you're welcome to drag your sorry ass down here and see for yourself."

Jim put away his walkie-talkie. Then, once and for all, he pushed aside any lingering worries about hotel-related problems. He had family to think about. Stuff that really *did* matter.

It was time to go meet Rayna.

CHAPTER

THE menaGerie, Part I

The hotel's parking garage contained seven levels, six above ground and one below. The cavernous underground lot accommodated tour buses, luxury motor coaches, and anything else that needed extra space and extra security. At night, a gigantic metal gate descended over the one and only entrance, locking it up tight.

Jim stood beside K-7, awaiting the arrival of his sister.

A voice crackled over his walkie-talkie.

"Here they come," said Oscar. "Holy shit. You are not going to believe this."

"Believe what?" Jim replied.

Almost before he got the question out, his sister's ride lumbered around the corner. It was an enormous recreational vehicle—the kind that rock stars use while touring and retirees take to Yellowstone. Only Jim had never seen one like this before. It was painted a shiny, metallic bluish silver. Something resembling a satellite dish sprouted from the grill. Along the entire length of the roofline on both sides ran fat metal tubes with flickering red lights at the front.

Jim knew exactly what he was looking at: a very costly, very elaborate, very pathetic attempt to turn the RV into the USS *Enterprise*.

"Houston, we have a freak show," he muttered dejectedly.

The RV came to a stop with a hiss of air brakes. The side door cracked open, and out jumped Rayna. She closed the ten feet between them in three excited strides and embraced him. He hugged her back, lifting her petite frame off the floor.

"You've changed," she said as she stared up at his face. "You look more serious."

"You have no idea," Jim replied. "But you've changed, too."

"Really? How?"

"You're blue. And you have antennae sprouting out of your head."

"I'm an Andorian," Rayna said. "We're a warlike race from an M-class moon. You can call me by my proper name, Lieutenant Thellina."

"Already got your geek on, I see."

"You should be congratulating me," Rayna said. "I've just been promoted to helmsman of the USS *Stockard*."

"What's the 'Stockard'?"

Rayna pointed to the RV.

"I see," Jim said. "Who gave you this rank?"

The door to the *Stockard* swung open again. Out stepped a tall, thin, twenty-something man wearing a gold jumpsuit with a matching gold jacket. He also had on aviator shades—the big ones that Tom Cruise sported in *Top Gun*.

"Hey, Lieutenant Hottie," he called. "Where'd you run off to?"

Jim watched as Mr. Ray-Bans put his left arm around his sister's neck. It wasn't a hug as much as a mock wrestling hold. For a moment he wondered if he was going to give her a noogie.

"Don't mess up my antennae," Rayna pleaded.

Jim felt his neck and shoulders stiffen. He'd only just met this guy, but he'd already disliked him for years.

"Matt, this is my brother, Jim," Rayna said.

"Matthew Stockard," he said. "Or rather, for the duration of this soiree, *Commodore* Stockard. Commander of the USS *Stockard*."

"Matt taught me how to drive this thing," Rayna chimed in.

"At first I worried she couldn't handle a big rig," Matt said. "But she's a natural. Real enthusiastic."

It occurred to Jim that he would have no problem putting Commodore Asshole on the garage's cement floor. He certainly had the means, and Matt just handed him the motive.

Rayna sensed her brother's mood. "What he means is, I drove most of the way here," she offered soothingly. "It's really not that hard."

"I'm sure it's not," Jim said. "What do you do for a living, Matt?"

"That's 'Commodore.'"

"Whatever. What's your actual job?"

Rayna frowned. "Jim, during a convention it's not good form to push people for details about their mundane lives," she said. "If they want to volunteer information, that's fine. But—"

"I'm a software developer for Imp Entertainment," Matt said. "Worked on a couple of games you've probably heard of. D'you know *Shopping Maul*?"

As a matter of fact, Jim did. He'd played the game several times. It featured a post-apocalyptic shopping center overrun with mutants. You had to go from store to store, buying things while wiping out the bad guys with a chain gun. It was actually pretty challenging. Shooting people while pushing a shopping cart took some getting used to.

"Sorry, it doesn't ring a bell," Jim lied.

A look of disappointment flashed across Matt's face.

"Your loss," he said. "It was only last year's hottest first-person shooter game."

Matt turned his hands into finger guns and pointed them at Jim's chest.

"Ka-pow!" he said. "Ka-pow! Ka-pow!"

Then he raised the finger guns to his mouth, blew away imaginary smoke, and pretended to holster them.

Jim tried to think of something to say. He was saved from the attempt when another one of Matt's passengers descended from the RV. She was Rayna's age and sported a bobbed black haircut and clunky rectangular glasses. Her uniform consisted of a halter top and miniskirt, plus pointed prosthetic ears and a dagger holstered on her right hip.

"Jim, this is my friend T'Poc," Rayna said. "T'Poc, Jim."

"Hey," T'Poc offered.

Jim heyed her back.

"T'Poc is a Vulcan officer from the ISS *Enterprise*, which exists in a mirror universe ruled by the barbaric Terran Empire," Rayna said. "You know, the inside-out dimension where all the good guys are bad guys and Spock has a goatee."

"Yeah," Matt said. "Get her drunk and she'll show you *her* goatee."

"If he's lucky," T'Poc smiled.

"That sounds . . . great," Jim said uncertainly. "What do you do in the real . . . "

Rayna shot him a look.

"I mean, what do you do aboard the evil, mirror-image *Enterprise*?"

"I'm the commanding officer's personal yeoman," T'Poc said. "I assist him in his amoral, selfish quest to claw his way to the top of the command chain. It's roughly analogous to the job belonging to my counterpart in this universe."

"And that would be?"

"She's my executive assistant," Matt said. "Keeps track of all the stuff I'm too busy to remember."

"Speaking of which," she said, "you need to get Gary off the ship. He's really stinking up the place."

Matt sighed, then pounded on the side of the RV.

"Hey Horta, get your pimply butt out here!" he shouted. "Front and center, mister, before Imp Entertainment decides to replace you!"

"Coming," called a voice from inside.

The door opened once more, and a grossly overweight young man climbed out. Unlike the others, decked out in their full convention splendor, he wore ratty jeans, faded yellow Chuck Taylors, and a threadbare shirt that read "I Stole a Bird of Prey, Resurrected Spock, and Saved the Planet, and All I Got Was This Lousy T-Shirt."

He also reeked of putrescence and was spattered with vile black goo.

"Meet Gary Severin, my pet Horta," Matt said. "You know what a Horta is?"

"Not a clue," Jim lied again, when in fact he knew all about the lumpy, silica-based, acid-spewing subterranean monsters that debuted in the classic *Trek* episode, "Devil in the Dark." But he played dumb, forcing Matt to spend more than a minute explaining the concept.

"I call Gary a Horta because he's large and lumpy, too," Matt concluded, just in case the comparison wasn't clear.

"I also suffer from acid reflux," Gary said forlornly.

Jim frowned. "Is that why you're covered in slime?"

Matt walked over to Jim and put his arm around his shoulders. He left it there, as if they were old friends. "Gary had a run-in a few miles back with a psycho soccer mom . . . or something."

"Or something?" Jim asked.

"He can tell you all about it. As a matter of fact I guarantee he'll tell you since he hasn't shut up for one goddamn minute since it happened. But never mind all that. Right now we need to find our rooms and change our clothes, because the Klingon Feast starts at ... T'Poc?"

"Seven o'clock in the Gweagal Room," the Vulcan said tonelessly.

"We'll be there ten minutes early," Matt decided, "so we can find a table big enough for all five of us."

Jim did the math and then shot a look at his sister, who seemed to have found something very interesting on the garage floor to observe. "You told me *we* were meeting for dinner at seven," he reminded her. "This was your plan?"

"I'm booked all weekend," Rayna apologized. "But I really want to see you."

"Trust me, you're going to love it," Matt said. "There's a bat'leth demonstration, barrels of bloodwine, and all the gagh you can eat."

"I don't want to spoil your Trek buzz," Jim said. "You go eat your gagh and have fun."

"Please come," Rayna said. "For me?"

"Actually ... "

"Did I mention that Matt has been hitting on me nonstop for the last three hours?"

"I'll be there," Jim decided. He retrieved a trio of room keys from his pocket and distributed them to Matt, Rayna, and T'Poc. "You're all checked in," he explained. "Just take the elevators over there. Gary and I will take the freight elevator way over *there*, so he won't scare off the paying guests."

"Where are the elevators?" Matt asked, his head swiveling around. "I don't see them."

"Lose the shades," T'Poc said.

Matt, with great reluctance, finally took off his Ray-Bans.

"Ah, target acquired," he said. "See you later, Jim, Brother of Rayna. And here's something for your college fund."

He slipped a ten-dollar bill into the breast pocket of Jim's jacket.

Jim felt a flash of true anger. He was about to suggest someplace else where Matt could slip his money when, once again, he caught a glimpse of his sister. And he refrained. Instead, he grabbed Gary's duffel bag from inside the RV and then led him across the dimly lit garage toward the service elevators.

"Hey, Oscar," he said into his radio. "I've got my sister and her friends. Thanks for letting me know they were coming."

"Can't talk now, buddy," came the static-filled reply. "I got some knuckleheads causing trouble out here. Standing in the street. Harassing cars. Drunk frat boys, I'm guessing."

"You need help?" Jim asked.

"Go have fun with your sister," Oscar told him. "I've got this situation under control."

Jim clicked off his radio and turned his attention to Gary. "I don't mean for this to come out the wrong way," he said, "but is your buddy Matt as big of an asshole as he seems?"

"You ain't seen nothing yet," Gary promised. "Once he settles down at the Klingon Feast and has a few drinks, his douche-bag powers will go to full strength. He'll crank it all the way up to warp 9.95."

Jim assumed this was bad. Very bad.

The two plodded the rest of the way to the elevator in silence. Jim mused that there was an excellent chance, a truly excellent chance, that Matt wouldn't get out of the Botany Bay Hotel alive.

CHAPTER

THE CAGE

Meanwhile, in a distant level of the hotel far, far away, Princess Leia Organa lay handcuffed by the wrists to the headboard of a queen-size bed.

The man holding the key to her freedom was named Donnie Trill. He was a self-styled Web entrepreneur, videographer, and the closest thing she had to a confidant. They'd known each other for about a year. Whenever Trill needed a female model for one of his oddball Internet video projects—and had cash in hand—he gave her a call.

She watched as Donnie messed with the settings on his digital camera. He wore an ill-fitting gold uniform from the original *Star Trek* series. It stretched in a profoundly unflattering way over his gut.

But that wasn't what troubled her now. She was mulling over the larger issue of how she'd reached such a crossroads in her life. How a perfectly normal—well, *reasonably* normal—person such as herself wound up doing such patently abnormal things.

She'd been pondering that question a lot lately.

"Tell me again what this is for," she asked.

"Some fan site," Donnie said, not bothering to look up from his camera. "For people who despise the Star Wars franchise. Actually, it's for Trekkies who despise Star Wars."

"Does it have much of a following?"

"Just fifty thousand paying subscribers."

"Good Lord."

"You know what's really impressive? Their creative director pays cash up front. I'll send him the video tonight and it'll go live almost immediately."

"What do I have to do?"

"Just lie there. The premise is that you're a Star Wars groupie dressed as Princess Leia, and that I'm an obsessed Star Trek fan who's kidnapped you, handcuffed you to a bed and then . . . "

"Nothing sexual."

"Honey, have you forgotten who you're with?" Donnie said. "I'm gayer than George Takei. All I'm going to do is stand around and berate you about how much the Star Wars universe sucks and how Star Trek is superior in every way."

"And then what?"

"And then the Death Star explodes and the rebel base is saved. What do you think? I shut off the camera, unlock the cuffs, give you a thousand bucks, and we're done."

She sighed and rolled her eyes.

"How long will this take?"

"Maybe fifteen minutes. The guy gave me a script. You don't have any lines. Just look annoyed. Kind of like you do now."

"Well, hurry up. I've got another job right after this one."

"Booth babe?"

"What else? They've got this ridiculous outfit for me—a silver-blue bathing suit—and they want me to carry a spear. I'm playing Shahna from 'The Gamesters of Triskelion.'"

"I have no idea what that means."

"It's a classic Season Two episode. Kirk, Chekov, and Uhura are captured by disembodied brains who use them as gladiators—"

"Do you wear a wig?"

"A nice one," she said. "Platinum blonde. Very Lady Gaga."

"The fanboys are going to love that. Maybe you'll make a new friend this weekend."

"I'm just here for the money," she assured him.

She never had the interest nor the ambition to pursue conventional modeling—and at a healthy six foot one, she didn't exactly have a clothes-rack body. But at a small-scale event like GulfCon, she was invariably a belle of the ball. And when the fanboys discovered that she genuinely loved science fiction—that she could quote chapter and verse from *Deep Space Nine*, they'd plead to have their pictures taken with her. She usually worked two or three gigs a month and every dime went right into the bank.

She took a deep breath and closed her eyes. *Okay*, she thought. *Character. Get into character. If I'm going to spend the weekend as bikini eye candy for pervy fanboys, no one has to know who I am. As long as I'm wearing this getup, I am* Princess Leia.

"A lot of these guys have serious bank," Donnie remarked. "If you can look past the uniforms and the prosthetic ears, you could land yourself a really nice boyfriend."

"Just roll the camera, Dr. Phil."

"You don't want a boyfriend?"

"I don't want to talk about it." She fidgeted on the bed. The handcuffs were digging uncomfortably into the tender skin on her wrist. "The only person I like to depend on is me."

"Brrrrr, you're frigid tonight!" Donnie said, grinning. "But I'll tell you what. We're going to get good and drunk in the hotel bar tonight and work through some of your issues."

He turned off the ringer on his cell phone and set it down on the nightstand along with the handcuff key. Then he mounted his camera on a tripod, turned on its tiny auxiliary light, and looked at the preview screen again.

"Now when I start, I'll do a few seconds of you trying to yank your hands free. Then I'll walk in and start reading the script."

"You're just going to stand there and read?"

"Nothing in the contract says I have to memorize this. And no one's going to be looking at me, anyway. I could hold a rabid raccoon and people wouldn't notice."

Donnie shuffled through the several pages of typed, single-spaced dialogue. Then he cleared his throat.

"And what's with Jar Jar Binks?" he announced in a theatrical voice. "People say he's a walking, talking Happy Meal toy. But you know what? That's an insult to Happy Meal toys! They're way more entertaining than Jar Jar!"

"Is it all like that?"

"Pretty much. The guy told me to sound really ticked off."

"Your fury is almost palpable. Let's do this thing."

As Donnie switched on the camera, something thumped the wall above her head.

"What was that?" Leia asked.

"The people next door must be having a quickie," Donnie said. "Their timing sucks. It'll ruin the take."

A moan wafted through the wall.

"We can't wait for them to finish," Leia said. "I have to be down-stairs in—"

"I know, I know," Donnie said.

There was a second thump, followed by a short, high-pitched

scream.

"You need to shut them up," Leia said.

Donnie turned off the camera and its light and then started toward the door.

"Hey, I was kidding," she said. "Don't you dare leave me like this."

"Hold tight," Donnie said. "I'll just be a second."

He opened the door and stepped out into the hallway. He pulled the door closed behind him, but it didn't latch. Instead it bounced against the frame and then drifted open a couple of inches.

Leia tested the handcuffs to see if she could slip free, but Donnie had tightened them all the way.

Thanks, buddy, she thought.

A few seconds ticked by. Then a few more. She glanced over to the key on the nightstand. It was just eighteen inches away from her right hand—but it might as well have been a mile.

"Donnie?" she called out.

He didn't reply.

The seconds stretched into minutes.

Leia considered calling out again, but the noises coming from the adjacent hotel room made her think better of it. There were more moans—but not the sort you'd expect to hear under such circumstances. There was no pleasure in these voices. They sounded like they were dying—or worse.

Even more troubling, the voices seemed to be moving into the hallway. The stretch of hallway just beyond her slightly open hotel room door.

Leia didn't know what was happening, but she knew she wanted no part of it.

She lay perfectly still, using a yoga technique to calm her breathing, hoping that Donnie would return, but gradually understanding that, for whatever reason, he wasn't coming back.

I've got a bad feeling about this, she thought.

CHAPTER

5

ERRAND OF MERCY

The service elevator was big and poorly lit. Some of the hotel staff used it for cigarette breaks, so it normally reeked of smoke. But today all Jim could smell was Gary. Or, rather, the black viscous goo on Gary's T-shirt.

The elevator's doors slid shut. It slowly rumbled up toward the seventh floor.

"You'll have to forgive me for asking," Jim said, "but what the hell happened to you?"

"Crazy shit is what happened," Gary explained. "We were heading down 249 and were just inside Beltway 8 when the Commodore stopped for gas. You can probably guess who had to pump."

Jim pointed at Gary.

"Affirmative. Now the only other car in the gas station is a Volvo station wagon. And while I'm standing there waiting for the RV to tank up, I realize the driver of the Volvo isn't moving. She's slumped over the steering wheel. Her window's down maybe six inches. The stink coming out of this car is unbelievable."

"What did you do?" Jim asked.

"I tap on the glass and there's no response. So I figure she's dead.

I've found a dead body. I call out for Matt to come look, and in that split second the woman is suddenly grabbing me. Her hand's through the open window and she looks nuts. Her face is smashed up against the glass and her mouth is snapping like a crocodile's. That's about all I remember. Matt says I did some crazy, girly-looking dance until she let go."

"He didn't get out and help?"

"Nah. He said he felt obligated to stay clear, because he'd heard on a National Geographic special that you're not supposed to screw around with nature's rhythms. So he just sat there watching me while I fought off that crazy bitch."

"But the stuff on your shirt—"

Gary nodded.

"It was all over her hands. Actually, I'd swear it was coming *out* of her hands. Like blisters or lesions or something. They were all over her face, too."

Jim studied Gary's face for a moment. Then he let out a long sigh.

"That sounds like Dawn of the Freaking Dead," he said. "You sure you aren't jerking my chain?"

Now it was Gary's turn to study Jim.

"You got me," he said. "It's all a joke. I rolled in roadkill, just so I could get you to believe my story about being attacked by an insane milf in a Volvo. Because even though we've only just met, I *live* to jerk your chain. I fantasize about it."

The elevator bell rang for the seventh floor and the doors slid open. Jim stepped out first to make sure the hall was clear.

"All right," he said. "Let's go."

"I wouldn't worry about scaring the guests," Gary told him as he emerged from the elevator and followed Jim down the hall. "I won't be the weirdest sight at a Star Trek convention."

"Maybe not," Jim said as he stopped in front of room 744. "But you're definitely the weirdest smell."

He passed the room card over the door, unlocking it. The accommodations included two queen-size beds, a small bathroom, and windows overlooking the Botany Bay's vast atrium. Over each bed hung a painting—the same paintings that could be found in the majority of the Botany Bay's guest lodgings. One showed Captain Cook landing for the first time on the Australian coast—at a place he'd soon name Botany Bay. The other showed his sailing ship, HMS *Endeavour*, in storm-tossed seas. The paintings were the hotel's most obvious— and pretty much only—attempt to explain its name to patrons.

Though why a hotel in Houston would choose for its theme the adventures of an eighteenth-century British sea captain was beyond Jim.

"Thank Surak!" Gary exclaimed. "All I want to do is lose these clothes, grab a shower, and have a long, long nap."

"The first two are on the agenda, but not the third," Jim said as he dropped his companion's big, green duffle bag on the bed. "We're due downstairs for the Klingon Feast."

Gary looked at him wearily and then unzipped his duffle bag, fished out a large, cardboard shirt box and a shaving kit, and disappeared with them into the bathroom. A few moments later the toilet flushed. Then the shower kicked on.

Jim flopped into a tiny upholstered chair near the windows. He made a mental note to ask Gary to put his funky clothes in a plastic sack, so they didn't stink up the place. He contemplated stepping out into the hallway and mooching a garbage bag from a housekeeping cart.

Then he pushed the idea from his mind. Why should he give a damn if one of the hotel's rooms smelled? Or, for that matter, if a

Klingon battle-cruiser cake was delivered? Or if the catering staff abandoned their posts?

None of it was life or death.

But that business with the woman in the Volvo. That *was* life and death. It added to Jim's general sense of unease. People bitten. People sick. A woman moaning and biting and reeking of death, just like *Dawn of the* . . .

Gary emerged from the bathroom wearing a stupendously ill-fitting blue-and-black jumpsuit. The sight utterly derailed Jim's train of thought.

"First-season *Next Generation*," Gary said. "My mom made it for me. What do you think?"

It looked to Jim like the Starfleet recruiters were really scraping the bottom of the barrel, but he tried to frame his appraisal more diplomatically. "I'm probably the wrong person to ask," he said. "I feel like I outgrew Star Trek a few years ago." Then he gestured at Gary's crotch. "But your sack is, like, *right there*."

Gary tugged resolutely at the suit's inseam.

"Better?" he asked.

"You might want to do that every few minutes. Just to be safe."

Gary sat down on the corner of the bed.

"I'm whupped," he said.

"Maybe the zombie milf infected you," Jim suggested.

"Dude, I never said she was a zombie. That's *you* talking."

"But think about it. She tried to bite you," he mused. "She was obviously out of her mind. And at least *some* of that slime on your shirt is blood. I've seen enough to know the look. And the smell."

"Now you're freaking me out," Gary said.

"I'm freaking myself out," Jim said. "But I know two people who were bitten today. One of them developed a really strange rash on her shoulder. And a lot of my coworkers are calling in sick. Isn't this how zombie movies always start? With lots of minor, seemingly unrelated incidents?"

"There's just one problem with your theory," Gary said. "Zombies don't exist. Those movies are fiction."

"I know," Jim said, "but the data all points to the same conclusion."

"The same highly illogical conclusion," Gary clarified. "Speaking as someone with a really tenuous hold on reality, I think you might want to take yourself offline and undergo a full diagnostic, if you get my drift."

I'm not the one in a form-fitting jumpsuit, Jim thought, but he didn't see the point in debating it further. He didn't really believe that the world was being overrun with walking dead—he just knew that his instincts were buzzing, and he was desperate to understand why.

But first, they had a feast to attend.

Jim and Gary left the room and headed down the hallway toward the elevators. Gary quickened his step when he realized it was almost seven o'clock. "I don't need any shit from Matt for being late," he said.

"Relax," Jim said. "Why do you put up with him?"

"Matt can be a real jerk, but he's already a legend in gaming. You'll see tomorrow at the autographing session. He'll have fans lined up for hours. I guess it goes to his head sometimes."

The elevator arrived and they stepped inside. "Being talented is no excuse for treating your employees like dog shit," Jim said.

Gary sighed. "He's actually *my* employee. I'm his boss."

"Seriously?"

"It's like this," he explained. "Thinking up a fresh, hugely popular game is hard. Designing one is even harder. Matt thought of one and also designed it. That means he's valuable and has to be tolerated.

My job—one of my biggest jobs—is keeping the talent in my company happy."

The elevator descended smoothly and quickly. Its glass walls offered a panoramic view of the Botany Bay's vast lobby.

"You're a professional punching bag," Jim said.

"An extremely well-paid professional punching bag," Gary said. "But I'll give Matt some credit: at least he doesn't make stuff up. He says I'm fat, and I am. He says I can't get a date, and I can't. He says I live with my mother, and I do."

"If you're so well paid, why don't you get your own place?"

Gary's face suddenly grew serious.

"Look, Mom's sixty-seven years old and she's been confined to a wheelchair since I was in high school. Ever since . . . the accident. She tells me I should get my own place, live my own life, but I can't just dump her in a rest home and walk away. I want to take care of her, the way she used to take care of me. Do you understand?"

"Yeah," Jim said. "Actually, I do."

"Awesome. Because I just made all that shit up. My mom is healthy as hell. I live with her because I'm a social cripple."

Jim smiled.

"And I thought Matt was a jerk," he said.

The elevator dinged, announcing their arrival on the lobby floor. Gary started to exit, but Jim stopped him with an arm across the chest.

"Sack," he said.

Gary adjusted himself once more, and then they were on their way.

WINK OF AN EYE

Jim pointed Gary toward the Gweagal Room and then detoured to the Botany Bay's front desk. He found Janice at the counter, all by herself.

And none too happy about it.

"Why are you still here?" he asked.

"Dwayne hasn't come in," Janice said. "And his phone's out of service, or something. I can't reach him."

"Isn't there anyone else?"

"Would I be standing here if there was?"

Janice gave Jim a long, appraising look. He thought he could hear the wheels in her head turning.

"I suppose *you* could fill in," she finally said.

"Can't," Jim said. "I have a thing."

"Oh, a thing," Janice repeated testily. "What's her name?"

"It's not like that. My sister is here for GulfCon. I'm meeting her at the Festival of Klingons, or whatever it's called. I can't get out of it."

He backed his way down the hall before she could press him further.

"Way to take one for the team," she called after him.

Jim had no idea what took place at a Klingon Feast, but he had assumed it would be a little livelier than the scene he discovered in the Gweagal Room. It was in one of the Botany Bay's smaller meeting areas and seated 150 guests for receptions, banquets, and corporate functions. Tonight, Jim pegged the head count at fifty, sixty tops. Most were either huddled around the bar or clustered in tight groups at tables. A few wore various iterations of Starfleet crew uniforms. The rest were done up in leather or faux leather and carrying fake blades.

In one corner, several Klingons were engaged in a head-butting contest, slamming their cranial crests together like rutting mountain goats. And over by the bar, someone pounded out a monotonous Klingon opera on a synthesizer keyboard. A few onlookers sang the libretto in guttural, artificially low baritones. Jim's understanding of the Klingon language was sketchy, but he recognized the words "fight," "kill," and "death" in the lyrics.

He surveyed the banquet table, laden with Terran approximations of various Klingon delicacies. The sights and smells ranged from exotic to flat-out disgusting. Among the more palatable items were krada legs (smoked turkey), pipius claw (conventional crab), and heart of targ (a quivering, livid, red Jell-O mold).

Two men in full Klingon drag bellied up to the buffet. One grabbed a mock krada leg and took a hearty bite.

"How is it?" Jim asked.

"Bland," the Klingon replied. "Needs more crapok sauce."

Jim grabbed what he hoped was an ordinary cheeseburger and then set off for the large, round table where Matt, Rayna, Gary, and T'Poc were already eating. Sitting across from them were a knot of Klingons.

As soon as Matt caught sight of Jim, he glared at him.

"Dude, what kind of shithole is this place?" he asked.

"Excuse me?" Jim said.

"This is the worst Klingon Feast in five years of GulfCon. Look at all the empty chairs. You can't even get a plate of gagh."

Now that *was* strange, Jim thought. Sarah Cornell had seemed determined to pick up those gummy worms, but apparently she had never made it back from the warehouse club.

"We were expecting up to three thousand walk-ins," Jim said.

"Three thousand, my ass," Matt said.

Jim surveyed the room. The gathering didn't look very festive. From what he could tell, there were only two distracted-looking servers. Ordinarily, for a dinner banquet in a hall this large, there would be seven.

"Maybe everyone has con plague," said Rayna. "Too many people, too many germs, too much alcohol, and not enough sleep. I had it pretty bad in San Diego last year. I spent the last two days of that show flat on my back, fighting a virus."

"Or maybe," Gary said, delaying his response for maximum dramatic impact, "it's the zombies."

"What?" Rayna and T'Poc exclaimed simultaneously.

"Jim was talking about it earlier," Gary said. "He thinks Houston's been overrun by zombies."

"I didn't say *that*," Jim corrected. "I just said a zombie outbreak would explain some of the strange things that I've seen today. Two of my coworkers were bitten. The cops have been crazy busy. Some psycho lady smeared blood all over Gary's shirt. This is not a normal day."

"You know zombies don't exist, right?" Rayna asked.

"I'm not the one with antennae sticking out of my head," he reminded her. "Don't accuse me of having an overactive imagination."

It was a slightly awkward moment, but T'Poc jumped in to defuse the tension.

"Bring on the braaaaains!" she cheered. "I'd rather deal with the undead than a bunch of *Babylon 5* fans!"

Everyone at the table, Klingons included, voiced their hearty approval.

"Most sci-fi conventions cover all the bases these days," T'Poc told Jim. "But GulfCon's just for Trekkers."

"Now that's something I've never understood," Jim said. "Is there really any difference between a Trekker and a Trekkie?"

The table erupted in conversation. Several people tried to answer at once, but Rayna's voice won out.

"Everybody's got their own opinion about this," she said. "Some people consider 'Trekkie' to be a derogatory term coined by those who don't understand the scene. They think it denotes someone without social skills who gloms onto Star Trek as a sort of substitute life."

"Trekkie," Matt shouted, pointing at Gary.

"Asshole," Gary responded, pointing back at Matt.

"I get it," Jim said. "So what's a Trekker?"

"A Trekker is someone who tries to live by the philosophy and ideals espoused in the Star Trek universe," Rayna said.

"Like what?" Jim said. "Paint yourself blue? Wear shiny clothes?"

"Like, believe in the perfectibility of the human race," Rayna countered.

"Or that tomorrow will be better than today," one of the Klingons added.

"Or that by working hard, we can bring real and lasting change," Gary said.

Jim resisted the urge to laugh at their naïveté. There were times when he felt compelled to describe the horrors he'd witnessed in Afghanistan. Decimated villages. Shattered limbs and burned bodies.

Little children who looked as broken and shell-shocked as grizzled combat veterans. These sights didn't fill him with confidence about the future of the human race. But as usual, he kept his mouth shut, and the conversation turned to other subjects: the Gamma Quadrant, the *Voyager*, Leonard Nimoy's career as a director. He decided to get up and walk to the bar. The two servers working the room were running themselves ragged, and Jim knew he'd get a drink quicker if he ordered it himself.

"You want a Klingon martini?" the harassed-looking bartender asked him. "They're gin and vermouth with a shot of bloodwine."

"What's in the bloodwine?"

"Everclear and red food coloring. It's really popular tonight."

"I think I'll just have a Bud," Jim decided. "Make it a pitcher."

He returned to the table and offered the beer to the group. His new friends cheered—all except Matt, who appeared preoccupied with watching the entrance to the Gweagal Room. After everyone had a glass, Jim asked Matt if he was looking for someone in particular.

"I'm supposed to meet a Klingon," Matt explained. "He makes edged weapons. I ordered a bat'leth from him. All custom work. Made a fifteen-hundred-dollar down payment."

"I know that guy," Jim said. "I think I met him right before you showed up."

"Well, he was supposed to be here ten minutes ago," Matt said. "If he stole my down payment I'm going to kick his ass."

T'Poc answered with an amused snort. "Have you *seen* Martock? He's, like, seven feet tall. The guy's muscled up like an Augment."

"And he's got enough knives and swords to arm an entire boarding party," Jim added. "He'll carve you up like a serving of bregit lung."

Laughter rippled around the table.

"Screw you guys," Matt said. "I'm a central character. Nothing bad is going to happen to me."

"You're a what?" Jim asked.

"I'm the star of this show," Matt explained. "Flag personnel in the various *Star Trek* series never get killed."

"What about me?" Gary said. "Can I get killed?"

"Much as I hate to admit it, you're probably safe, too," Matt said. "You're the comic foil. The funny characters always live to see another episode."

"And me?" Rayna asked.

Matt furrowed his brow.

"It doesn't look good," he said. "The commander's romantic interests are always transitory. You're slated to die in a horrifying final plot twist."

Matt moved on so quickly that he didn't notice the irritated look on Rayna's face.

"I know where *I* stand," T'Poc said. "I'm a semiregular character, like Guinan on *Next Gen*. I don't even have to die. I could vanish tomorrow and things would go on without me."

"That about sums it up," Matt said.

Jim took a swig of his beer. "Think about this," he proposed. "What if you're *all* extras? Do you know how many starships, with their captains and their yeomen and their crusty doctors and their comic relief guys, got blown to bits during various *Star Trek* episodes? Maybe you're one of *those* crews. Maybe you're all just phaser fodder for some other set of characters that truly matter to the story."

Jim took another drink and let the Trekkies mull it over.

"Dude, that's deep," Gary finally said. "We go around thinking we're the big dogs, but maybe we're all just crewmen on the USS *Constellation* or the USS *Bellerophon* or the USS *Yamato*. We exist simply to die. We make some minor plot point, then get dispatched."

"Heavy," T'Poc said.

"Bullshit," Matt said. "I'm not an extra. I'm in the goddamn opening credits."

Jim was still formulating a response when a female Klingon returned to the table from the bar, cursing under her breath.

"Party's over," she said. "They just ran out of bloodwine and they aren't getting any more."

"What?" Matt said.

He directed a glare at Jim, as if he were personally responsible.

"Fine with me," Gary shrugged. "I need some sleep."

"You can sleep when you're dead," Matt said. "Let's go up to my room and par-tay."

Jim couldn't believe that anyone was still using the word "par-tay" to describe an experience that was supposed to be enjoyable. Even the Klingons at the table seemed skeptical. They looked at each other, then at their watches.

"We're just going to call it a night," one of them said. "We were supposed to do the bat'leth demonstration, but two of our guys got caught up in a riot. Down by the train station, I guess. They wanted me to pick them up, but no way am I driving in this traffic."

"Did you say riot?" Jim asked.

"*They* said riot. It sounded like a riot."

"Maybe it's the zombies," T'Poc laughed. "Or wait—maybe it's vampires! The sun's set and now they're finally making their move!"

Gary and Rayna laughed. Jim didn't.

He knew people didn't toss out the word "riot" in idle conversation. Cell phone reception was bad, but it wasn't *that* bad. The kid with the toy phaser had complained that his television didn't work. There was no signal. Just static.

Jim's instincts were screaming. He still couldn't grasp the threat's true nature, but he sensed its silhouette. And it was enormous.

He told Rayna that he was going to swing by the front desk to check with the manager.

"You do that," Matt replied. "Tell them that the VIP in room 754 is having a meltdown about the shitty service. Use those exact words, okay?"

"Got it," Jim sighed. "Meltdown. Shitty service."

They rose from the table en masse. Their move triggered a general evacuation of the banquet, with everyone heading somewhat listlessly toward the doors.

"You will come by, right?" Rayna said.

"Count on it," Jim said. "Watch yourself until I get there."

"Watch myself? What am I watching for?"

"Trouble."

"Are you okay? You're acting kind of paranoid."

"Something's going on. I'm not saying it's zombies, but it's something. I've felt it all day. Now, suddenly, it's worse. So keep your head on a swivel."

He watched as the group started down the hallway to the lobby. He hung around for a minute, waiting to see if anyone would appear to clean up the mess. No one did. Even the two servers seemed to have vanished.

Finally he stepped out into the hallway, turned out the lights and locked the door behind him. Jim closed his eyes and then slowly rolled his neck from right to left.

He opened them just in time to see Martock running out of the men's room and heading toward the lobby. He was still in full armor and full makeup but moved with an urgency that didn't look like playacting. Jim was about to call out to him when he noticed something on the carpeted floor.

Something red.

Something wet.

Footprints.

Jim followed them to the door of the restroom. It was located halfway down the long hallway that linked the lobby to the Endeavour Room. He stepped cautiously up to the door and, not knowing what else to do, knocked. No one answered.

He took a deep breath and pushed it open. It resisted slightly. He heard something metallic scrape across the floor.

"Hello?" he called as he entered. "Everything okay in here?"

A quick glance downward revealed that everything was, in fact, *not* okay. The scraping sound had come from a bat'leth lying on the floor. Jim figured Martock had dropped it on his way out.

The blade was covered with blood.

Jim stepped over it and entered the bathroom, backtracking over the Klingon's crimson footprints.

"Anybody in here?" he called.

A bank of toilet stalls to his right prevented him from gaining a full view of the room. Jim stepped around them cautiously until he reached the row of sinks and urinals in the back.

A blood-drenched body lay in a thick, red-black pool of rapidly congealing blood.

"Hotel security," Jim said, inching closer. "Are you okay?"

He realized the body wore the same dirty athletic shoes he'd spotted on the woman sleeping in Martock's booth.

Then he realized the body was missing a head.

Jim reeled back toward the sinks, managing to catch one to balance himself. Fighting nausea, he tried to put everything together in his mind. The Klingon had decapitated her with his bat'leth, then dropped it at the door and run away.

He turned around and stared at the mirror. There was a large, crimson smear in the middle of the glass. Jim looked into the sink beneath it.

The bloody face of a young woman stared up at him.

The rational part of his mind told him that the force of the decapitation must have bounced the head off the mirror and plunked it into the basin. The primal part shouted for him to get the hell out of there. Now.

For a moment, reason kept control. Jim gazed down at the face. There was an odd, purplish growth right in the middle of her forehead—just like the welt he'd seen on Sarah's shoulder, only larger, roughly two inches in diameter. Otherwise he could swear it was the exact same mark.

Jim leaned closer to study it.

Suddenly the growth popped open, revealing a glaring, fully developed eye. It peered directly at him.

All pretense of reason fled. Jim leapt away, caromed off the bathroom stall behind him and ran out the door as fast as his unsteady legs could carry him. He didn't stop running until he reached the front desk.

CHAPTER

7

A TASTE OF ARMAGEDDON

Jim found Janice standing behind the counter, utterly alone.

"Call the cops," he told her. "Now."

"The phones aren't working," she said. "I can't get through to anyone."

"Did you try your cell?"

"No service. Nothing works."

Jim gasped for breath.

"Dexter," he said. "Is Dexter still around?"

"I don't know."

"What about Oscar?"

"He went out front twenty minutes ago."

"Why?"

"Because I asked him to. Ever since the sun went down, people have been walking outside to get better reception on their cell phones."

"So?"

"After a while I realized that none of them were coming back."

Jim's breathing began to steady. He slowly got himself under control. As he did, he realized that something about Janice had changed. She didn't seem angry or put-out or frustrated anymore. She seemed frightened. Profoundly and deeply frightened.

"Oscar didn't come back, either," she whispered.

Jim looked out the glass doors. All he could see was darkness.

"All right," he said. "I'll take a quick look—"

"No!" Janice said. "Didn't you hear what I just said? Nobody comes back!"

Jim hesitated. The crime scene he'd just witnessed had rattled him to his core. But seeing Janice—confident, dogmatic, in-control Janice—coming unglued was almost worse.

"It'll be okay," he said. "I'll just stick my head outside. You'll never lose sight of me. Sit tight."

Jim headed toward the doors. Then he stopped and turned around.

"One more thing," he said. "I need you to do me a favor. My sister, Rayna Pike, is staying on the seventh floor. I want you to call her and tell her to stay in her room. She needs to stow her Star Trek crap for a while and look after herself."

Janice stared back at him. He wasn't sure if any of his words had registered, and there wasn't time to repeat them. He stepped through the first set of glass doors, into the main entrance's air-lock.

The doors shut behind him, leaving Jim, finally, with a fairly decent view of the outdoors. The Botany Bay was located on the edge of downtown Houston, just minutes away from the city's convention center and financial district. Aside from the occasional fanboy convention, the hotel mostly catered to business travelers. The surrounding neighborhood offered little in the way of tourism or nightlife. There was an Applebee's down the road, and a Starbucks that closed at eight o'clock, but the rest of the avenue was given over to generic office buildings and parking garages. Tonight the streets and sidewalks were empty, just like any other night.

Jim glanced back into the hotel. Janice was behind the desk, staring at him. He waved at her, smiled, then opened the exterior door and stepped outside.

A blast of hot, humid Gulf Coast air washed over him. He looked west, then east, and saw nothing unusual. Off in the distance, maybe two blocks away, he made out a pair of pedestrians. But something was wrong, and it took him a moment to realize what was missing.

Smokers. On any normal night, one would find a knot of guests and staffers puffing away in front of the hotel, near the entrance to the alley where he'd spotted Rodriguez earlier in the day. It was the Botany Bay's unofficial nicotine refuge. Midday or midnight, rain or shine, there were always smokers.

Except now.

Jim took a few hesitant steps toward the alley. He noticed a pack of cigarettes lying on the ground. And an iPhone. There was also a purse.

And a smear of black liquid that might have been motor oil.

Jim took a few more careful, quiet steps. He was close enough to hear noises coming from the alley. Footsteps shuffling. Voices grunting. Something ripping.

The homeless men and women he'd glimpsed earlier in the day, hiding in the shadows at the far end of the alley, were now just around the corner from him. And their numbers had grown. They sounded like an angry mob.

For a moment he contemplated simply confronting them. Until he remembered that this was probably what Oscar had done. Oscar the ex-Marine who was now MIA.

This isn't in my job description, Jim thought. *I'm just the goddamn bellhop.*

He retraced his steps to the hotel entrance, keeping a careful eye on the alley's mouth. He was almost to the doors when he realized the two pedestrians were now much closer, less than a hundred yards away. They were walking so strangely. Staggering, really. Just like zom—

No, he thought. Rayna and Gary were right. Zombies did not exist.

But these two people—whatever they were—were definitely staggering toward him. They'd seen him and were coming his way as fast as their wobbly legs could carry them.

As Jim watched, he became aware of gunshots in the distance— the *pop-pop-pop* of a semiautomatic pistol, followed by a staccato blast that could only be produced by a fully automatic AK–47 assault rifle.

All of a sudden, Houston sounded like A-Bad on a Saturday night.

CHAPTER

THAT WHICH SURVIVES

Jim couldn't remember the last time Janice Bohica greeted him with a smile. But tonight, when he reentered the lobby, she did just that. She seemed almost hysterically relieved to see him.

"You came back," she said.

"We've got a problem," he said. "Isn't there a button under the counter that locks these doors?"

"Yes, but it's only for emergencies."

Jim nearly said something mean but looked into Janice's eyes and restrained himself. Everyone in the hotel would need to stay calm. As soon as people panicked, they would be no help at all.

"This *is* an emergency," he said, keeping his voice under tight control. "I guess you could call it a riot. And a couple of the . . . of the rioters . . . saw me and they're heading this way. We need to secure the doors."

Janice reached beneath the marble countertop and punched several digits into the keypad. "I haven't used this code since the Astros lost the World Series. I think it's 2063."

The keypad responded with three affirmative chirps and the front doors bolted with a loud *clunk*. Jim pulled on the three interior doors. They were all secure. He assumed the outer ones were locked, too.

Trouble was, they were all made of glass.

"Should I lock the other doors, too?" Janice asked.

"What other doors?" Jim said.

"All of them. All of the Botany Bay's exterior doors."

"You can do that? Nobody told me there was a code for *that*."

"Right after September Eleventh, the hotel got codes for everything."

"Use them," Jim said. "Lock us in."

Janice punched another set of digits into the keypad and the machine responded with three more chirps. Then Jim escorted her to Dexter's office. Halfway through the warren of cubicles, Janice stumbled and fell to her knees. Her breathing grew shallow and ragged. For a moment, Jim wondered if she was having a heart attack.

He knelt down beside her. "Are you all right?"

Janice pushed him away. "I just need a few minutes." When she finally looked up again, she examined the surrounding desks as if searching for a good place to hide.

"We don't have time for this," Jim said, forcing his arm around her waist and helping her to her feet. "Can you walk?"

"I'm fine," she insisted.

But he kept his arm around her waist, anyway. Her footsteps were slow and unsteady. As though she was quite literally buckling beneath the pressure.

Dexter's office was a rat's nest of forms, paperwork, and Dallas Cowboys memorabilia, but it also contained a few items that Jim desperately wanted. He found them sitting in a case—a case that, to his great relief, someone had opened and left unlocked.

Inside were two exotic-looking weapons. Their black-and-yellow color scheme made them look like gigantic bumblebees.

But with a much worse sting, Jim thought as he scooped them up.

"What are those?" Janice asked.

"Taser X3s," Jim explained. "The latest and greatest in less-than-lethal ordnance." Dexter had bragged about their capabilities on numerous occasions; they had laser sights, built-in LED flashlights, and a triple-shot capacity so that the user could fry three different people simultaneously. Jim considered showing Janice how the X3s worked and then maybe giving her one. But the flustered look in her eyes told him that wasn't an option. In her present state, Janice might even decide to taser *him*.

Jim located an empty black backpack and stuffed one of the weapons inside. The other he placed in a holster and latched to his belt. Then he found the black, circular Squad Charger that recharged the guns' battery packs. It held six fully topped-off power magazines. Jim slid one into his personal weapon and put the rest into the backpack. He noticed the toy phaser sitting on Dexter's desk and decided to grab it, too. Anything even resembling a weapon seemed comforting now.

"This feels like a dream," Janice said. "Can we go now?"

"One last thing," Jim said.

He went to the desk, opened the bottom drawer, and reached all the way to the back to the place where Dexter—in flagrant violation of hotel regulations—hid a 9mm Glock 17 pistol.

Usually, that is. But tonight all Jim found after an increasingly frantic search was a spare 17-round magazine, which he stuffed into his backpack.

"When was the last time you saw Dexter?" Jim asked.

"A few hours ago. There was a disturbance on the third floor, but he never came back."

"What time was that?"

"Just after five, I think."

Jim checked his watch. It was eight thirty, which meant Dexter had been out of contact for three hours and change. Maybe—hopefully—he was incapacitated somewhere. The alternative was too horrible to consider.

"Dexter, can you hear me?" he said into his walkie-talkie. "Are you okay?"

He tried twice more, and then put out a general call for someone, anyone, to respond.

There were no replies.

Jim closed his eyes and rubbed his temples. He had to get upstairs and find Rayna. He needed to see if perhaps, just perhaps, Dexter was still around. And then together they would set up a defensive perimeter and figure out a plan.

He offered a silent prayer that things wouldn't get any worse. A prayer that was immediately and decisively rebuffed.

"What's that noise?" Janice asked.

It was coming from the lobby. Someone was pounding on the doors. Pounding so hard that they rattled.

He glanced over at Janice. Her face had gone pale and her pupils were dilated. Her reason was now in full retreat, routed by the din in the lobby. There was no way to bring her along, not unless he was willing to carry her.

"Janice, I need you to do me a favor," Jim said calmly.

She nodded ever so slowly.

"I want you to lock this door when I leave and wait for me. Don't go out front, don't wander around. Just sit in this chair and wait. Will you do that?"

Another slow nod.

"Great. I won't be long, all right?"

No nod this time. Just a stare.

"Okay," Jim replied on her behalf. "I'll be right back."

He shouldered the backpack and walked out the door.

"No," Janice whispered after he departed. "You won't."

9

HOPE AND FEAR

As Jim walked through the hotel's offices toward the front desk, the banging from the entrance grew louder and louder. He got down on his hands and knees, crawled to the end of the check-in counter, and peeked around the corner.

He could just make out what he figured were the two pedestrians he'd seen on the street—a young man and woman, both fairly well dressed, looking something like a couple that had been out on a date. Now they pounded on the glass with bloody fists, creating large, smearing circles of red and black. Their loud, strange moans made Jim's neck hair stand up.

But that wasn't the worst.

There weren't just two of them anymore. There were at least a dozen, all in roughly the same sorry condition as the first pair.

One, a middle-aged man wearing the remnants of a UPS uniform, had taken what looked like a point-blank shotgun blast. A vast, bloody crater had been scalloped out of his chest. Another seemed to have extricated herself from a flaming car wreck. Her clothes were charred and smoking, her hair singed away, her body covered with livid-red burns the exact shade of barbecued brisket. Crawling underneath them was a corpse with no legs, dragging itself along on its hands.

No such thing as zombies, my ass, Jim thought.

He knew now that his instincts had been right all along. Something had happened. This *was* Dawn of the Freaking Dead. The end of the world was upon them, and his poor kid sister had no idea.

He forced himself to focus his thoughts. One thing at a time. First, find Dexter and secure the perimeter. Then get the remaining guests—especially Rayna—into a safe position where they could plan their next move.

Jim scuttled down to the far end of the check-in counter. He took a deep breath, calmed himself, then stood up and walked, as nonchalantly as possible, toward the elevators. They were only about a hundred feet away, but it felt like a hundred miles.

Maybe they won't notice, he thought as he stepped out into the open.

They noticed. Jim's sudden appearance set off a chorus of moans. The glass took an even more vigorous pummeling, but he knew it would hold. It was bullet-resistant and half an inch thick. The zombies could beat on it all day to no effect. The only thing capable of breaking the glass would be a moving vehicle, but driving one seemed beyond the capabilities of the gang out front.

Jim's legs felt like noodles as he closed the last few steps to the elevators. He pressed the call button and waited.

And waited.

At first he tried not to look at the entrance. But curiosity—and his own sense of self-preservation—won out. If one of those things somehow got through, he didn't want to have his back to it.

So, while the elevators took their sweet time descending to the ground floor, he looked.

When he did, his stomach rolled.

It's the gang from the alley, Jim thought. *It's all the people who went out to smoke or to make a phone call and never came back.*

Among the crowd he recognized Kai Opaka—or rather, a middle-aged woman dressed in the elaborate vestments of Bajor's supreme spiritual leader. She wore a purple robe and headdress, but the lower half of her jaw had been torn away, opening her neck and exposing the knobby ridges of her spine. And there was the boy who'd been playing with the toy phaser, the one who complained about the bad TV reception. Someone had plunged a carving knife into the side of his neck, and yet still he walked.

An elevator announced its arrival with a ding. Jim could barely hear it over the noise from the crowd.

He stepped aboard and hit the button for the third floor. Glancing around, he found everything was still as it should be. No broken glass, no blood on the floor, no abandoned personal items.

The doors slid shut, silencing the moaning and the pounding. In its place, all he could hear was Nichelle Nichols singing her cover of "That's Life."

Everything felt normal. For a moment—and for the last time—Jim allowed himself the luxury of imagining that perhaps things weren't as bad as they seemed.

That feeling lasted exactly as long as it took the elevator to reach the third floor, and for its doors to open.

10

DAGGER OF THE MIND

Back on the first floor, Janice sat in Dexter's office, impatiently tapping her foot. She stared at the clock on the wall, watching the second hand sweep through minute after uneventful minute.

The interlude allowed her time to think. Which, in her current state, was the most dangerous thing she could do.

The hotel staff had vanished. So had most of the guests. The phones didn't work. There were riots—or something like riots—in the streets. And now Jim had left her alone.

She looked at the clock again. Every time the red second hand reached the top of the dial face, the minute hand snapped forward with a pronounced *click*. She'd never noticed that sound before. How could she have never noticed?

As she stared at the clock, her subconscious mind made a decision. Instead of trying to make sense of the whirl of events, it simply pushed them away. The evening's growing list of horrors and mysteries were gathered into a tight ball and sealed inside a brittle shell of denial.

Denial and delusion.

"I'm the day manager," Janice told herself, as if suddenly remembering. "I've been doing my job for seventeen years and I've got a hotel to run."

Everything else was deleted.

She turned her attention to the racket in the lobby. People wanted in. Paying guests. They were probably angry. And it was her responsibility to help. Or at the very least explain what was wrong. Communication was often the key to soothing unhappy guests. People were surprisingly forgiving of subpar service when they understood the circumstances. The best way to earn lots of one-star reviews on travel Web sites was to keep your customers in the dark about problems.

Yet here she was, the day manager, parked in a chair because some kid told her not to move.

It didn't make sense. None of it made any sense.

All she had to do was take charge.

Janice got up, took a deep breath, and gathered herself.

"Everything will be fine," she thought. "I just have to face the problem and deal with it."

She left Dexter's office, walked slowly through the Botany Bay's abandoned administrative center and into the lobby. Her arrival set off a thunderous round of moaning and pounding.

She walked up to the interior doors. Close enough to get a good look at the crowd outside. She saw several of the costumed Star Trek people. They looked like they'd been in some sort of accident.

Her mood improved a bit when she spotted Oscar.

"Oscar!" she shouted over the din. "Are you all right? Where have you been?"

Oscar, she plainly saw, was not all right. There was blood all over his face, and something had opened up his torso and caused his intestines to spill out. The gray entrails dragged behind him like a tangled garden hose.

It occurred to Janice that he should seek medical attention, not stand outside pounding on the glass with his brawny arms.

Clearly something had to be done.

She thought of her training, of the management seminars she attended twice a year at the company headquarters in Charleston. Then she cleared her throat and began to speak.

"Ladies and gentlemen, I'm sorry to announce that your rooms are unavailable," she told the bloody horrors clambering outside. "The Botany Bay Hotel and Conference Center was founded on the promise of delivering excellent customer service to our guests. I realize we are failing to deliver on that promise, and I ask for your patience and forgiveness as we work to rectify this situation."

Janice was answered with more moans.

And with something else.

She heard it not with her ears, but with her mind. Not words but rather a powerful urge percolating up from the dark regions of her brain. Something was in there, telling her to do things. Implanting in her a strong, almost primal urge to unlock the doors. To allow the Botany Bay's poor, shamefully inconvenienced guests to enter.

She wondered where the suggestion might have come from. Was someone in the mob speaking to her? She looked from one bloody face to the next. All seemed to share the same peculiar type of growth, either on their faces or shoulders or, in one case, right in the middle of the chest. The bulbous masses looked like big, white eyeballs, but with crimson pupils in the middle.

All of the hundred or so people outside seemed to have them.

And every one of those eyeballs was staring at her.

Janice observed a woman dressed in a red Starfleet uniform. Pressed against the glass by the throng, she happened to be the creature closest to her. There was an eyeball sprouting out of her right shoulder. Janice looked at it closely. Very closely.

She gazed at it for several moments, transfixed.

The eyeball was trying to make contact with her. It wanted her to do something, but struggled to find the words. Finally, by ransacking what remained of its host's mind, it made its point.

We mean you no harm, it whispered to Janice's fragile consciousness. *Lower your shields.*

CHAPTER

11

DEVIL IN THE DARK

As the elevator arrived at the third floor, it occurred to Jim that he should unclip the Taser from his belt. Just in case. He switched off the safety and checked to make sure the weapon was loaded—and found that it wasn't. He'd forgotten to snap in a dart cartridge.

A moment later the doors slid open. The elevator emitted a *ding* loud enough to alert everyone—and everything—in the general area.

Out of instinct, he pointed the weapon anyway. Not that he could see much. Someone or something had knocked out the landing lights. He was greeted by a wall of darkness. He activated the Taser's LED flashlight and played it across the floor. It landed on an enormous bloodstain surrounded by bloody footprints. Someone, probably several someones, had died on that spot. But where were the bodies?

Things aren't as bad as they seem, Jim thought. *They're worse.*

Holding the elevator door open with his foot, he continued panning the light across the floor. It landed on Dexter's Glock 17. The hotel security chief's much-loved sidearm lay abandoned just outside the door to room 301.

Jim poked his head out of the elevator, wondering if he should press his luck and grab the pistol. All of the hallway lighting sconces were dark, but there was enough light from the glowing emergency exit signs to determine that the hall was currently empty.

The gun was no more than fifteen feet away. He desperately wanted it.

Jim sorted through his hotel passkeys until he found the one that overrode the elevator's computer. He pushed the card into the control panel, then locked the lift in place with its doors open.

Then he walked over to the Glock and picked it up. It was definitely Dexter's weapon. And it had been fired. Jim pulled the clip and discovered that only seven of its seventeen rounds remained. The security chief hadn't gone down without a fight.

Not that fighting did him any good.

Jim stood in the darkness, feeling his testicles trying to crawl up inside his body. He hadn't felt so unnerved since combat. Back then it happened mostly on patrol. Poking around strange houses and claustrophobic neighborhoods, he'd wonder if the next corner he turned would be his last.

This was very much the same feeling, only worse. At least in Afghanistan he wasn't alone. Now he faced danger all by himself.

Which is probably for the best, considering my track record, he thought grimly. *If I screw up here, nobody dies but me.*

"Time to boldly go someplace else," he muttered.

He was retrieving his passkey from the elevator control panel when a voice cried out to him.

"Hello? Is someone there?"

Jim was so startled he dropped the passkeys on the floor. He quickly gathered them up before stepping back into the hallway.

"Where are you?" he called.

"Room 308."

Jim's heart sank. The room was more than halfway down the hall to his right.

"Are you hurt?" Jim said.

"No, but I can't move. It's complicated."

Jim pointed the Taser's piercing beam down the hall. It was so intense that he feared it might give away his position. And he was already worried about running down the batteries. Then he remembered the plastic phaser. He removed it from his backpack and squeezed the trigger. The toy produced a less piercing but still helpful beam of amber light.

He holstered the Taser and then advanced with the pistol in his right hand, the phaser in his left. As he passed the doors to the intervening rooms, he could hear the occupants on the other side, groaning and gurgling and scratching at the doors. In their current state, they obviously lacked the smarts to work the doorknobs and get out.

Someone had used a room service tray to prop open the door to room 306. Jim paused before the threshold and peeked around the corner. He saw a middle-aged man in a bathrobe milling around listlessly between the room's two beds. A man with two bloody stumps where his hands used to be. And a grotesque third eyeball perched, somewhat impractically, on the top of his bald skull.

The creature seemed to notice Jim. It turned in his direction and bowed—presumably to give the eye on its head a better look. Jim didn't wait for the moaning to start. He reached inside and pulled the door closed.

Then he advanced to room 308 and discovered that this door was also slightly ajar. He wondered, briefly, if this was a setup. Maybe some of the zombies were smarter than others.

But he knew he had heard a human voice. Its desperation couldn't be faked.

Before entering, Jim pointed the phaser to his right and left, down both lengths of hallway. Still no contacts.

He shouldered the door open a few inches. It made a creak that Jim imagined could be heard all the way to Dallas. He pushed it open a couple more inches. Then a couple more. Then he slid in, the Glock leading the way.

The room was profoundly dark, save for the light from Jim's phaser. From the doorway he could see the end of the first bed.

A woman's bare legs lay across it.

Pistol ready, Jim walked down the short entry hall and played his light over the mattress. He found the legs' owner—a beautiful woman dressed in a golden metal bikini and a red silk loincloth.

"What the hell?" he said.

"Shut the door," she hissed.

Jim turned back to close the door and tripped over a tripod, knocking it and the attached camera to the floor. Then he pushed the door shut, locked it, and turned on the bedroom lights.

"Is there a key?" he asked.

"Right here," she said. "On the nightstand."

Jim grabbed it, climbed onto the bed, and inserted it into one of the cuffs. As soon as he unlatched the first cuff, the woman pulled her hand free, grabbed the key, and unlatched the second herself. Then she jumped off the bed in one athletic bound.

"Where are you going?" he asked.

"Where do you think?"

She disappeared into the bathroom and closed the door.

Jim tucked the phaser back into his belt, set the pistol on the end of the bed, and looked around the room. Aside from the video camera and the tripod, he didn't see any personal belongings—nothing, that is, except for an eight-foot length of chain that was draped across a dresser. He lifted one end, expecting a plastic prop, but the links were genuine steel and very heavy. Martock would have approved of its craftsmanship.

He turned on the television but there was no picture—just static. Then he turned it off and tried the telephone instead. He was still pushing buttons when the woman emerged from the bathroom.

"Anything?" she asked.

"No," Jim said, hanging up. "Not even a dial tone."

"We need to find someone who works for the hotel," she said. "Something weird is happening. You wouldn't believe some of the stuff I've heard in the last three hours." She went over to the window and opened the curtains, but all this revealed was a partial view of the parking garage across the alley.

"I *am* with the hotel," Jim said. "My name's Jim Pike and I—"

"Tell me what's going on."

"I could tell you, but you'd never believe me. You need to see for yourself, Ms. . . . "

The woman stood in front of the mirror over the dresser, quickly weaving her long, raven hair into a ponytail.

"Call me Leia," she said.

And all at once it clicked into place: the chain, the metal bikini, the red loincloth. She was dressed as Leia Organa in the opening scenes of the *Return of the Jedi*, when the princess was held captive as Jabba the Hutt's slave aboard a floating barge.

"Wow," Jim said. "Do *you* ever have the wrong hotel."

The woman laughed bitterly.

"Ya think?" she asked.

"We're going to be okay," Jim assured her. "My sister's some-where on the seventh floor, and once we find her we can—"

"You can do whatever you want," she said, heading for the door.

"I'm going straight to the lobby and getting the hell out of here."

She turned the latch before Jim could stop her. Instantly the door burst open, pinning Leia against the wall. In lumbered Dexter—or rather, all that remained of him. Something had gouged huge portions of flesh from his face, arms, and legs. He lunged past Leia and made straight for Jim, grabbing two fistfuls of his red jacket and shoving him backward onto the floor.

The weight crushed the air from Jim's lungs. He forced both of his hands around his attacker's neck, struggling to keep Dexter's furiously snapping teeth away from his face. But gravity worked against him. And there was something else. Something slimy on the security chief's neck kept him from getting a firm grip. It wriggled and twitched whenever Jim's fingers made contact.

It was an eye, he realized. An eye that had sprouted right where the Adam's apple used to be.

Trapped between the bed and the wall, pinned by his attacker's immense bulk, Jim knew he had only moments to live. Dexter's ravenous jaws were less than an inch from Jim's cheek.

And then, suddenly, they weren't.

Through a haze of panic he glimpsed Leia above him, looping a length of chain around the undead creature's neck. Then, straddling the two of them, she pulled with all her strength.

The force snapped back Dexter's head, freeing Jim's hands and allowing him to crawl out from beneath his attacker's body. He staggered to his feet, grabbed his Glock from the bed and leveled it at the horror on the floor. Leia kept pulling as hard as she could, every muscle in her body straining.

Jim was about to shout for her to stand clear when he realized shooting the thing wasn't necessary anymore. The creature formerly known as Dexter went limp. Jim advanced cautiously on the bloodied remains. He tapped the head, then the torso, with his foot. No reaction. Only then did he close the door and sit down on the corner of the bed, his pistol gripped loosely in his hands.

Leia dropped the chain and stepped back, gasping from the effort. "Next time . . . ," she began.

"Next time we'll check the peephole," Jim agreed. "It's a deal."

Too stunned to do anything else, Jim stared at the mess on the floor. He noticed a viscous green fluid oozing from the front of Dexter's neck. From precisely where the third eye had been.

"Is that a zombie?" Leia asked.

"I'm afraid so," Jim said.

"I didn't think you could strangle a zombie."

"I'm not sure you did. This particular zombie had some sort of third eye over its windpipe. Once you crushed it with your chain, it stopped moving."

Leia took this information in remarkably good stride. Jim knew that most civilians would respond just like Janice—their minds, numbed by panic and fear, would simply seize up. But Leia seemed focused, not terrified.

"I suppose there are more downstairs," she said. "That would explain all of the screams I've been hearing."

"There are quite a few," Jim said.

"And the police?"

"No police, no cell phones, no Internet, and no TV. Aside from my boss, you're the only person I've seen in the last hour."

"Then I guess we're on our own," Leia said.

There was a sudden loud pounding at the door.

"Not necessarily," Jim said.

He stepped up to the peephole and looked outside. Somehow the fight with Dexter had drawn the attention of more zombies. Jim could make out three of them, pressed against the door. He guessed there were more behind them.

"What now?" Leia asked.

"I'm thinking," Jim said.

"Some rescue," Leia muttered. "When you came in here, didn't you have a plan for getting out?"

"If you want to help, you can lay off the *Star Wars* dialogue," he said. "I've had enough sci-fi crap for one weekend."

"What dialogue?" Leia asked.

More pounding at the door interrupted his reply. Jim studied the lock and the hinges. It looked like it would hold—for now.

"Let's see what Dexter's packing," he said, and rolled the body onto its side.

Leia patted his belt and came away with a heavy flashlight, a can of Mace, and another black-and-yellow Taser X3.

"Do you know how to use that thing?" Jim asked.

"I own one," she replied as she checked the battery pack's power level. "A princess can never be too careful."

"What about shoes? You can't run around this place with bare feet."

"I don't have a choice. Unless you feel like running up to room 911 and grabbing my bag. In which case you could also grab my jeans, a T-shirt, and the bottle of ibuprofen next to the bathroom sink."

Jim opened up his backpack, snapped a cartridge into his own Taser, and stowed it in his bag. After a moment's consideration, he also dropped in the toy phaser. Then he offered a dart cartridge to Leia.

"Want a spare?" he asked.

"In a second," she said.

With considerable effort she reached underneath Dexter's immense body, undid his gun belt, and yanked it loose. It was more than a yard long—enough to wrap around her waist twice. Instead, Leia slung it over her right shoulder and fastened the buckle at her hip. When she reholstered the Taser, it rode just below her left breast. The Mace went into a pocket at her waist.

"Good to go," she announced.

"Works for me," Jim said, handing over the spare darts.

"So how do we get out of here? Shoot our way past the ones in the hall?"

"I've got a different idea." He pointed to the wall between themselves and the adjacent room 306. "Have you heard any noises in this room over the last few hours?"

"Not a peep unless you count all the moaning and screaming. That's why my friend Donnie went over to investigate. And he never came back."

Jim pointed to the opposite wall. "How about that room?"

"Silence," she said. "Seriously."

"It's probably vacant. Even with the Trekkies convention, this is a slow weekend for us, and this floor's only half-booked."

He shuffled through his passkeys, found the appropriate one, and stuck it in the interior connecting door's lock. He slowly pushed it partway open and shined Dexter's powerful flashlight inside.

"Anything?" Leia asked.

"Empty," Jim said. "No bags, curtains drawn, nothing out of place. We're good."

He walked toward the exterior door with Leia close behind.

"You're just going to walk out there?" she asked. "There could be hundreds of them."

Jim looked out the peephole. There weren't hundreds of zombies, but there were more than enough to give him pause.

"Wait here," he said. "And be ready to move."

He ran back into room 308, where the creatures were still pounding on the exterior door. This time, Jim pounded back.

"Hey, you stupid freaks!" he shouted. "We're in here! Tell all your friends!"

A chorus of moans erupted from outside. And then the pounding intensified. Furious and unrelenting. The metal portal shook on its hinges.

Jim waited a few moments. Then took several deep breaths, unlocked the bolt, and turned the handle. The door flew back instantly and slammed against the wall, pushed wide by the weight of the frenzied dead. Jim leapt away just in time to avoid the first wave of attackers. Caught off balance, they stumbled forward, falling in a pile at his feet. While others struggled to climb past them, Jim retreated to the connecting door and locked it.

He found Leia pressed to the exterior door, still watching developments through the peephole.

"Good idea," she said. "They're funneling right in."

Jim handed her the flashlight.

"We go when I say 'go,'" he said. "Once we're outside, click this thing on and aim it down the hall. Watch where you step. There's nasty stuff on the floor."

"Got it."

Jim checked his watch: it was well past nine o'clock. He could only hope that Rayna was still safe in her room. And that Matt didn't try anything stupid.

Jim clicked off the Glock's safety. Leia kept her post at the peephole.

"I think we're good," she finally said. "So far as I can see."

Leia stepped away. Jim unlocked the door and turned the knob. He opened it a few inches—just enough to make sure the coast was clear. Then he stepped outside. Leia was so close behind that he could feel her breath on his neck.

The zombies, apparently busy tearing apart the room next door, missed their departure. Leia clicked on the flashlight and guided their steps as they raced down the hallway. Upon reaching the elevator, they discovered that two zombies had beaten them to the lift. They stood on board, clawing with bloody fingers at the glass walls, oblivious to the potential meal standing directly behind them.

"Shit," Jim whispered.

"Double rat shit," Leia replied, reaching for the elevator call button. "Let's find another way down."

Jim grabbed her wrist, stopping her. "For all we know, the other elevators have more. We need to get rid of these two."

They heard a distant moan. They gazed down the hallway they'd just fled and saw nothing. But then Jim glanced at the opposite end of the hallway—the area he hadn't considered when formulating his escape plan—and spotted a half dozen zombies doddering toward them.

"We need to get rid of these two *right now*," Jim said.

"All right," Leia shouted. "Listen up!"

The two zombies ceased their clawing and turned as one. They began, ever so slowly, to stagger out of the lift.

Jim raised the Glock. It had been a long time since he had fired a sidearm at a moving target. He sighted the first zombie carefully and pumped a single round straight into its chest.

Nothing happened.

"You missed!" Leia said.

"I didn't miss," Jim said. "He just doesn't care."

He fired three more slugs into the creature's central body mass. Blood and black goo sprayed out its back, splattering the glass walls of the elevator, but the creature continued lurching forward.

"Do something!" Leia screamed. Jim could feel her fingers digging into his right shoulder.

The creature closed the final few feet between them. Arms outstretched, it drew near enough to smell.

Just as it prepared to lunge, Jim raised the Glock about a foot and fired a round into the monster's temple. It went down and stayed down.

"It's just like in the movies," he said. "You need to shoot the heads."

The second creature came close on its heels. Jim sighted its head, then changed his mind. Leia saw him waver.

"What's wrong?" she said.

"Nothing," he said. "Gonna try an experiment."

He fired at the eyeball protruding from the zombie's left shoulder. The round struck home. The creature collapsed just like the first one.

"Excellent," Jim said.

"What?" Leia said, her eyes riveted on the hallway zombies. "What's so excellent?"

"We've got two different ways to kill them," he said. "Things are looking up."

There was a shuffling sound behind them. Leia turned just in time to see the remains of Donnie Trill closing in. The once-chatty videographer now couldn't even manage a moan, having been relieved of his tongue and most of his nose and cheeks. Instinctively Leia pulled her Taser and fired. As soon as the electrodes connected, she turned on the juice. The creature collapsed, twitching violently, then lay still. The bulging eye on its right shoulder exploded in a burst of green goo.

Jim and Leia stared at it, slack-jawed.

"*Three* ways," she said, holstering her Taser.

They stepped aboard the elevator. On the sound system, Brent Spiner was singing "It's a Sin to Tell a Lie," with Jonathan Frakes and LaVar Burton doing the backup vocals.

"We need to go to the lobby," Jim said as he frantically worked the elevator controls. "I left the only other person I've found alive down there, and she's in a bad way. Mentally, I mean. We need to pick her up."

"Oh my God," Leia said, as she gazed out one of the glass walls. "Is that her?"

Jim peered through the streaks of blood and gore left by the zombies. He saw Janice standing in front of the main entrance doors, in full view of the monstrous, undead horde outside. A horde that had swelled to a horrific size.

There were no longer just dozens of zombies howling and clambering to get in. There were hundreds. Maybe thousands.

And Janice seemed to be talking to them.

CHAPTER

12

THE ENEMY WITHIN

Jim didn't grasp the full scope of the horror until he ripped his gaze away from the main entrance and studied the windows of the rooms overlooking the lobby. Floor after floor, in one bedroom after another, he saw freshly risen zombies pressed against the glass, pounding furiously, driven to a frenzy by the sight of Janice.

"We've got to stop her," he told Leia.

He punched the elevator's lobby button.

"Hurry," she said. "Those doors can't hold."

"They'll hold," Jim said. "They're tempered glass. And if they break through the first set they still have to deal with the second."

"Who's she talking to?" Leia said.

Jim looked out the window. Something about Janice's body language, and the way her head bobbed, suggested that she was indeed having a conversation. But that was impossible. There was no one to talk to. No one even capable of speech.

"What's she doing?" Leia asked.

Janice nodded one last time, then walked back toward the reception desk. The elevator reached the lobby and its doors opened.

"Stay here," Jim said, passing his backpack to Leia.

He ran out of the elevator as Janice felt beneath the reception desk for the security keypad.

"No!" Jim yelled. "Wait!"

She didn't hear. Aroused by the sight of another fresh meal, the undead created a storm of noise that drowned out everything else.

Jim remembered the pistol in his hand, raised it over his head and fired. The noise echoed off the hotel's marble-floored atrium. Janice heard the shot and finally glanced his way. She saw him and frowned reproachfully. Her lips moved:

Where were you?

Jim tried to speak. Nothing came out.

Then she said something else. Something that didn't make any sense.

The hotel's front doors sprang open. A tidal wave of bloody monstrosities surged into the Botany Bay. Janice, grinning as if she were welcoming a busload of charter tourists, stood her ground until the dead washed over her.

"No!" Jim yelled.

The wave broke over the hotel's front desk, submerging Janice beneath a sea of ravenous dead. The stench of decomposing flesh filled his lungs. Jim pointed the Glock into the crowd and squeezed the trigger. All he heard this time was a *click*. The gun was empty. He was still staring down at it when a hand grabbed his left shoulder and spun him around.

"Come on!" Leia screamed.

He ran on unfeeling legs back to the elevator, which was propped open with a plastic, potted ficus tree. He kicked it out of the way. The doors closed just as the first of the zombies smashed against the clear panels that surrounded them on three sides.

"Get us out of here!" Leia shouted as face after hideous, hungering face pressed against the glass.

"It's okay," Jim said matter-of-factly as he locked the doors. "They can't get to us. On the ground floor we're surrounded on the see-through sides by a thick Plexiglas sheathing. It's to keep people from getting crushed by the elevators. It also makes a pretty good zombie barrier."

Then he slumped down onto the floor, dropped the Glock and put his head in his hands.

"There was nothing you could have done," Leia said, trying to ignore the horrors surrounding her.

"There's never anything I can do," Jim said. "Never a goddamned thing."

"What happened?"

"She let them in. She unlocked the doors and let the zombies in."

"Why?"

"Maybe she got tired of waiting for me to come back," Jim said.

"What did she say to you?"

"The last thing she said before she opened the doors was, I believe, 'I have to lower the shields.'"

"Are you sure?"

"Pretty sure. What the hell does that even mean?"

The zombies slammed against the Plexiglas with enough force to make it shudder.

"I don't know," Leia said, a look of mounting panic in her eyes. "All I know is that if you don't get this damned elevator off the ground, I'm going to go as crazy as she was."

Jim glanced over her shoulder to the zombies. He recognized several faces. One of the Klingons from the feast, his snapping-turtle headpiece now wildly askew. A uniformed member of the Botany Bay's housekeeping staff who had obviously made her last bed. The guy who brewed him a double latte every morning at the hotel atrium's coffee kiosk. Different people from different walks of life, but now with one thing in common. Each had a third eye located somewhere on the head or shoulders or arms or chest. An insane-looking eye with a crimson pupil.

He also noticed, in a detached way, that the ocean of horrors surrounding them seemed to mount higher and higher. The first arrivals, the clumsy bastards, were tottering and falling as new monsters pressed in. The newbies stood on top of the first wave. As the mound of the fallen grew, the zombies who stayed on their feet gained altitude.

It wouldn't be long, Jim mused, before they surmounted the elevator's protective sleeve and climbed onto the box itself.

And once they were *on* the elevator, they would be *in* the elevator.

Jim looked up at the access panel in the ceiling and wondered if he should prop it open and help the zombies along. Dying, even at the hands of flesh-eating ghouls, might be preferable to seeing Rayna and Janice in his nightmares. More accusers, asking him night after night why he let them down.

But Leia clearly had a different view. He could see it in her face—her beautiful, terrified face. She was still talking to him, and he tuned in for a moment.

" . . . can't make the buttons work because you've frozen everything with your passkey!" she screamed. "You need to get your shit together before they climb on the roof and trap us!"

"It's hopeless," he replied. "They're everywhere. They'll kill us no matter what we do."

"But they don't have to kill us *right now*!" Leia shouted. "We can hole up someplace, figure something out. Or maybe just die on our own terms. Wouldn't that be better than suffocating in this box?"

Jim thought about it. The woman made sense.

The zombie mound was almost to the top of the Plexiglas. Another minute and the first creature would thump down onto the top of the elevator.

"Let's go to seven," Jim said. "I hear it's nice."

"Anywhere," Leia said as she stared down at the floor. "Anywhere but here."

Jim pressed the appropriate code into the control panel and left the zombies behind. Leia shuddered as they cleared the writhing mass.

"I have a thing about enclosed spaces," she finally said. "Especially spaces enclosed by zombies."

The elevator stopped at seven, dinging to announce its arrival. The doors, at Jim's instruction, didn't open. They soon heard pounding and moaning from the other side.

"Sounds like a par-tay out there," Jim said.

"Par-tay?" Leia said, still trembling. "Who says 'par-tay' anymore?"

"You'd be surprised."

Jim tried to get the lay of the land by looking out the blood-streaked windows. With nothing to stimulate their appetites, the zombies in the lobby settled into a round of listless pacing. And the ones in the hotel rooms—the ones staring down at the atrium—also seemed calmer. The mess on the elevator glass made it nearly impossible for Jim and Leia to be seen.

"I think we're okay for the moment," Jim said. "But there's no way we can open these doors."

He picked up the Glock and ejected its empty magazine. He unzipped his bag, drew out the fresh clip, and slammed it home.

"Seventeen rounds left," he said as he looked down at the sea of undead. "I don't think that's going to be enough bullets for all of them."

"What the hell happened to you down there?" Leia asked.

Jim pushed himself into the corner of the elevator next to the control panel. He crossed his arms and stared off into the middle distance.

"What happened was, I made a mistake. I put someone in a situation that they clearly couldn't handle. And she died. She died because I was stupid."

"Save your existential crisis for later," Leia said. "Right now, we have to survive. We need a Plan B."

"Really?" Jim said. "I didn't realize there was a Plan A."

"There was," Leia said. "You thought it up. Go down to the lobby and fetch what's-her-name, then go upstairs and find your sister."

"What's-her-name was named Janice Bohica,'" Jim said. "She liked to play golf, she was pathologically afraid of spiders, and for some reason she followed the Astros. We didn't like each other very much. But she deserved better than this. And better from me."

"*No one* deserves this," Leia said, gesturing at the elevator's grimy windows. "But that woman is dead and nothing can undo it. Getting your drawers in a knot won't help you or me or your sister."

"Rayna's dead," Jim said. "I left her, too, and now she's dead. She was eaten alive in a hallway somewhere while I was nowhere in sight. That's how it works."

"We don't have time for this," Leia said impatiently.

Jim looked at her with true anger.

"How's this for a Plan B?" he said. "How about I put the barrel of this pistol in my mouth and pull the trigger? You can take the passkeys and the stuff in the bag and go your own way. Trust me, you'll live longer."

Leia stalked up to Jim and looked him in the eye.

"You have no idea how much I want to go my own way," she said. "But I can't do this alone. You know the layout of this dump, you know how to handle weapons, and you know how to fight. As much as I hate to say it, I *need* you."

"I'll get you killed," Jim said.

"I'll take the chance," Leia replied. "Now let's put aside your personal baggage and try to think about how Kirk would handle this."

"Who?" Jim said.

"James T. Kirk, commander of the USS *Enterprise*."

Jim shook his head.

"I get it now," he said. "I'm dead and in Hell, trapped for all eternity with a Star Trek nerd. We're going to spend the next thousand years debating whether the Squire of Gothos was actually Q in disguise."

"Just bear with me," Leia said. "Think this through for a minute. Do you remember the Kobayashi Maru test?"

"From *Wrath of Khan*," Jim said, nodding. "It's a Starfleet training exercise that always results in the 'death' of the test subject. It gauges a cadet's reaction to a no-win situation."

"Correct," Leia said. "But what did Kirk say about no-win situations?"

"He doesn't believe in them."

"So hopefully you see the relevance. To paraphrase Kirk, even when you think things are hopeless, they aren't. You're just missing something."

Jim didn't see the harm in playing along for just a minute.

"Okay, let's review," he said. "We're trapped in the elevator of a hotel that's filled with flesh-eating zombies. We can assume, based on the police being a total no-show, that we're in the middle of an entire city, maybe an entire nation, that's likewise afflicted. We have minimal weapons, no food or water, and no way to open these doors without being immediately attacked by an enemy with crushing numerical superiority. Correct?"

"Right," Leia said.

"So what have I missed?"

"Among a great many other things, you've overlooked the fact that the zombies are morons. You're ready to throw in the towel to creatures who can be outsmarted by doorknobs."

"Valid," Jim said.

"And it's not like they're invincible. We already know three ways to stop them. Bullet to the head, bullet to the third eye, Taser shot."

"Affirmative," Jim said.

"And here's the most important thing. You're clumsy, you're slow, and you don't seem terribly smart."

"Right," Jim said. "Wait, *what?*"

"I mean that we're nothing special. If we made it this far, others must have, too. They're out there, and your sister could be one of them. We won't know until you get it in gear."

Jim uncrossed his arms, pushed away from the elevator's corner, and stood on his own two feet.

"I still think you'd be better off if you ran away," he said.

"You're the one who wants to run away," Leia replied. "But it isn't going to happen. People need you, and they don't stop needing you just because you wish they didn't."

"Well, I'll try not to disappoint."

"Do, or do not," she said. "There is no try."

Jim placed his right hand on Leia's bare shoulder.

"What did I say about the movie talk?"

Leia brushed his hand away.

"I'm not movie-talking anything. I'm trying to get us out of this situation, and you're the one who keeps bringing up . . . "

The elevator's emergency phone rang.

They both looked at it, too stunned to move. When it rang again, Leia lunged for the receiver and put it to her ear.

"Hello?" she asked breathlessly.

She listened for a moment, then, with a trembling hand, gave the phone to Jim.

"It's for you," she said.

13

strategem

Jim took the phone.

"Who is this?" he asked.

"This is Lieutenant Thellina, helmsman of the USS *Stockard*."

"Rayna!" Jim exclaimed. "You're okay?"

"I haven't been eaten yet, if that's what you mean. How are you and the princess?"

"You can *see* us?"

"Barely, with all that zombie blood and goo stuck to the elevator. Look out the panel to your right."

Jim gazed through the glass at the bank of seventh-floor windows, peering from room to room. Zombies in the first. Zombies in the second. Zombies in the third and the fourth and the fifth—and then two very-much-alive Trekkies waving frantically for his attention.

"I see you," Jim exclaimed, waving back. "Is everyone okay?"

"Everyone except T'Poc. She's dead, Jim. A bunch of those . . . creatures . . . it happened so fast, like a stampede. They trampled her. Matt saw the whole thing. He said it was awful."

"Just hang in there. I'm coming to your room."

"Then you better talk to Gary. He's getting ready to barricade our door. Let me put him on."

"I'll be there as soon as I can," Jim promised.

"Right," Rayna said, though it wasn't entirely clear that she believed him.

A moment later, Gary was on the line.

"Where'd you find the princess?" he asked.

Jim ignored the question. "Is your room secure?"

"It seems to be. There's no immediate threat now that we're behind locked doors. The only problem now is that we can't get out. The hallway is absolutely crawling with .... with ...."

"We've decided to go ahead and call them zombies," Jim said.

"You nailed it, buddy. I'll never doubt your weird hunches again."

"Is anyone else with you?"

"Matt."

"Seriously?"

"Yeah," Gary replied glumly. "Go figure."

"How did you find us?" Jim asked.

"Rayna noticed that woman standing at the front entrance, so I tried to call her. I was dialing the desk number when we spotted you down there. Which was really ballsy, by the way. We all kneel down before your mighty and monumental sack."

"That's possibly the grossest compliment I've ever received," Jim said.

"Normally, I can do a lot worse," Gary replied. "But I'm preoccupied right now."

"Have you been able to reach the outside world?"

"I've tried, but so far, no dice. Nothing but snow on the TV. Phones are toast. And no Internet, which is really strange. It was originally designed to serve as a fail-safe communications mode during a nuclear war, so it's very, very resilient. To lock it down this tight, you'd have to have someone very smart and powerful actively denying service."

"Or maybe it's gone," Jim said.

For a moment the line was silent.

"What?" Gary finally said. "What do you mean?"

"Maybe it doesn't exist anymore. Maybe it suffered some sort of catastrophic, worldwide failure."

"Oh, no," Gary said with disturbingly brittle finality. "That's not possible. Somebody's keeping us from getting to the Internet, but the Internet is still there. It will always be there."

Jim decided to back off. Given the stress that Gary already faced, implying that the Internet was dead might do him in. Besides, there were more urgent things to worry about.

Five minutes earlier, Jim's "plan" had been to put a gun in his mouth and surrender to the undead. But now that Rayna was safe, the gears in his head once more started to turn.

"You're in Matt's suite, right?" Jim asked. "Room 754?"

"You can't miss it," Gary said. "It's the room with all the zombies out front."

"Are they banging on your door?"

"Not really. They're just walking around in the hallway. It's like they sense that we're close, but they're not sure how to find us."

"Good," Jim said. "Then don't build any barricades because I need to get in your room. When you hear a knock, look through the peephole to make sure it's us, then let us in."

"Uh-huh," Gary replied skeptically. "And when do you see this happening?"

"We're getting ready to start right now," Jim said as he pressed buttons on the elevator's console. "Expect us in twenty minutes if things go well. If things don't go well . . . just keep somebody by the door until we get there."

"Rayna will do it," Gary said.

"Good choice," Jim replied. "Do you have any weapons?"

"Nothing yet, but I do have the walkie-talkies from the *Stockard*."

"That's even better," Jim said, and he gave Gary instructions for using the hotel frequency. "See if you can reach me."

The almost-forgotten walkie-talkie in Jim's jacket pocket beeped for attention. He fished it out and clicked it on.

"Dead Meat Two, this is Dead Meat One. Come in," Gary said.

"Excellent," Jim said as he hung up the phone. "Now we can contact you anytime. But for the time being, don't try to contact *us*. We might be sneaking up behind a lot of zombies so we don't need you spoiling our surprise. We'll check in when we can. Got it?"

"Got it," Gary replied. "Oh, hey, Matt wants to say something. You got a minute?"

The walkie-talkie changed hands before Jim could answer.

"Hey Jim, brother of Rayna," Matt said. "This shit's like *Resident Evil*, know what I'm saying?"

"This isn't a game," Jim said. "Your friend T'Poc is dead."

"I did everything I could to help that girl," Matt said. "But when you're facing down a dozen enemy combatants, there's not a lot of options. *You* know how it is."

Jim let the remark slide. He was pretty confident that Matt had never faced any adversaries outside of a PlayStation game, but there was no point in challenging him.

"Is there something important you wanted to tell me?"

"Just that we've got everything nailed down in here. Your sister's in good hands. *Really* good hands."

Jim felt his neck muscles tense.

"We'll talk about it when we get there," he said. "And don't get too comfortable. We're not staying."

"Says who? The minibar's got a couple days' worth of snacks and booze. By that time, the National Guard or the Marines or the Texas Rangers or whoever's in charge of quelling zombie outbreaks will have fumigated the place. Meanwhile, we'll sit tight and par-tay."

Leia shot Jim a look. "Par-tay?" she whispered.

"I don't think we can count on other people helping us," Jim reasoned. "If help is on the way, they're not going to prioritize the Botany Bay over hospitals, schools, government buildings—"

"Sorry dude, but this is my crew, and the decision's been made. You're welcome to come aboard for a visit, as long as you respect my orders. And those orders are to abandon the saucer section, raise shields to maximum, and wait for help. Now talk to Horta."

The walkie-talkie changed hands again, and Gary was back.

"You need to get us out of here," he whispered. "I think Matt's having trouble."

"What kind of trouble?"

"He's acting funny. I'm not sure I can explain it. But he barely blinked when T'Poc went down. I'm not sure her death even registered. Like he was just playing another game of *Shopping Maul*."

"Keep an eye on him," Jim said. "Watch for suspicious behavior. And grab the pens off the hotel desk. If you get in a tight spot, you can use them as weapons. Eyeballs. Windpipes. Anything soft and fleshy."

"You're freaking me out," Gary said.

"We're just warming up," Jim said. "See you soon."

The walkie-talkie clicked off and Jim pressed the elevator button for the eleventh floor.

"What's on eleven?" Leia asked.

"Remember how I said the hotel wasn't crowded? It got me thinking. The eleventh-floor common areas are being painted. Which means they stink. Which means we wouldn't put anybody up there unless we had to. And because it's a slow weekend, we didn't have to. I think it's empty. We can walk to the end of the hall and take one of the fire stairwells down to seven."

"What if those things are in the stairwells?"

"One problem at a time," Jim shrugged. "We'll kill the zombies if we have to, but we'll try to avoid them. Keep moving and keep quiet. This ammo might have to last us a long time, so I don't want to waste a single bullet. If you need to drop a body here or there, use the Taser. The Glock is noisier, so it doesn't come out unless we're well and truly boned. Okay?"

"You sound like you've done this before," Leia said.

"Not exactly," Jim said. "But after two tours in Afghanistan, I've become pretty good at sneaking around dark, dangerous places."

The elevator arrived at the eleventh floor. Jim and Leia pulled their Tasers, walked to the back of the elevator, and stood shoulder-to-shoulder. Jim hit the button and opened the doors.

"All right," he said. "Let's get this par-tay started."

14

THE FORGOTTEN

The doors parted to reveal a landing filled with ladders, scaffolding, paint cans, and drop cloths. The lights were undamaged and functioning. There were no suspicious stains on the floor. The only odor was the reek of fresh paint.

Normal, Jim thought. *Totally normal.*

But he kept his Taser in hand just the same. So did Leia.

"Just like you figured," she said, surveying the landing. "Empty."

"I'll bet the painters were up here just a few hours ago," Jim said. "Probably went downstairs at quitting time and walked out to their cars, thinking it was just another day. . . ."

"Don't dwell on it," Leia said.

Jim holstered his Taser and poked around among the paint cans.

"What are you looking for?" Leia asked.

"These guys usually wear junk shoes at work. Sometimes they take them home, but if they know they're coming back, they leave them. Maybe, if I can find a pair that's not too funky . . ."

"Don't worry about funky," Leia said. "I'll wear anything I can squeeze on my feet."

Jim spotted something. He walked behind a scaffold and returned holding a pair of ratty, paint-encrusted high-tops.

"Here you go," he said. "I hope they're comfortable."

"I'm a woman," Leia said as she sat down on the floor and slipped her toes into the sneakers. "I've never owned a comfortable pair of shoes in my life."

Jim watched as she tried to force them on. By his estimation they were almost an inch too short. But he said nothing. Better, and far safer, he calculated, to let Leia make the journey from denial to acceptance all by herself.

It took about ninety seconds.

"Dammit!" she shouted as she hurled the shoes across the room.

"I'll look for more," Jim said.

He resumed rooting around among the drop cloths, slowly making his way from one work area to the next.

"Hey," he finally called from across the room. "I think I found another pair."

"Do they look bigger than the first ones?" Leia asked.

"Shit," he said. "Actually, they look like they're attached to someone."

Leia leapt to her feet and ran to Jim's side, Taser in hand.

"What is it?" she asked.

Jim stood over a rolled-up drop cloth. Protruding from the end were two black, ankle-length boots.

"We may have a problem," he said.

"Zombie?" Leia said.

"I don't think so. The zombie wounds don't stop bleeding. But this drop cloth looks clean. Not a speck of blood."

"But someone wrapped him up," Leia said. "Why?"

Jim was about to hazard a guess when the back of his neck started to tingle. Someone or something was behind him.

"Look out!" he shouted as he spun and pointed his Taser. Leia went down on one knee and brought hers to bear, too.

They found themselves pointing their stun guns at a thin, sandy-haired man in his mid-twenties. Eyes wide with surprise, he stood with his right hand extended, as if he'd been about to tap Jim on the shoulder. He wore a Star Trek uniform from the original series—black pants with a red tunic.

"What are you doing to Olson?" he asked.

Jim and Leia maintained their stances a moment longer until realizing that—since the kid could talk—he couldn't possibly be a zombie. And since he wasn't a zombie, there was no reason to shoot him.

They sheepishly holstered their weapons.

"Who's Olson?" Jim asked.

The kid pointed to the body on the floor.

"We came for the convention," he explained. "I'm Ensign Willy Makit."

"Willy . . . Makit?" Jim asked. "I'm guessing that's not your real name."

"Of course not," Willy said. "It's my character's name."

"What are you doing all the way up here? I thought we had most of the GulfCon guests on the lower floors."

Willy's shoulders rounded as he dropped his head.

"The hotel said it was a simple mistake, but I believe we were intentionally segregated," he said. "We wanted to be with everyone else, but I think word of our group got around and no one wanted to stay near us. So the hotel put us here. We didn't find out until we arrived."

"I don't understand," Jim said.

"I do," Leia said. "Are you part of a red-shirt group?"

"I'm the last surviving member of the West Texas Red Tunic Club," Willy said. "A once-proud organization formerly boasting a membership of eight."

"Where are the other seven?" Leia asked.

"Dead," Willy replied, his voice cracking. "They're all dead. One insane, stupid accident after another."

"There's nothing accidental about these zombies," Jim replied. "Once you understand their behavior, it's very easy to predict everything they're going to do."

Willy shot him a puzzled look.

"Zombies?" he asked. "What zombies?"

The question hung in the air for a moment. He appeared to be serious.

"Oh boy," Leia whispered to Jim. "This is bad."

"Have you been up here the entire evening?" Jim asked.

"Yes."

"Have you, at any point, glanced out a window and seen the lobby?"

"Yes."

"So when you saw that the hotel was filled with bloody, mutilated, reanimated corpses, did it occur to you that there might be some sort of emergency?"

"I figured it was a costume party," Willy shrugged. "Or maybe a flash mob? The truth is, I had bigger things to deal with. Like seven of my friends dying in one day."

Jim looked around the hallway, astonished. "Are you telling me that you managed to lose seven people while holed up in the only secure space in this entire building?"

To Leia and Jim's extreme unease, Willy covered his face with his hands and began to cry. For a long, long moment it was the only sound on the eleventh floor.

"It's these uniforms," he finally choked out between sobs. "*They* killed us. They're cursed. And I'll be the next victim."

"You need to back up a minute," Jim said. "You think you've an-gered some kind of Star Trek deity by wearing a red uniform?"

Willy took a moment to compose himself.

"In the original *Star Trek* series," he explained, "the characters dressed in red tunics were always doomed. If one beamed down to a planet with Kirk and Spock, the guy in red would always, *always* die. So my friends and I decided to, you know, *celebrate* that by form-ing a club. It seemed like a good idea at the time. We'd all come to GulfCon in matching red shirts. We'd say we were the crew of the USS *Expendable*. It would be hilarious, because in the real world nobody dies just because they wear the wrong costume to a sci-fi convention, right?"

"That's right," Jim said impatiently. "Here in the real world, peo-ple don't die just because they wear a red shirt. That's crazy."

"I thought the same thing when I woke up this morning," Willy said. "I drove up for GulfCon with Olson, Carlisle, and Henderoff. The rest of our club was driving up a few hours later because they had to wait for Leslie to finish her shift at Best Buy. We were all going to meet at the Klingon Feast. But after we arrived and settled in, I got a message saying that our second crew was killed in a highway acci-dent. A tractor-trailer collision. They hadn't been on the road fifteen minutes when it happened."

"Oh, my God," Leia said. "I'm so sorry."

"We were all in shock. And the fact that we couldn't get a de-cent phone connection to anyone back home just made things worse. We thought about leaving, but it was getting near sundown and we didn't want to risk driving after dark."

"Because you were afraid something would happen to you too?" Leia asked.

"That's right. The idea of a red shirt curse had been funny before, but now not so much. Especially to Carlisle. He was accident-
prone to begin with. Always tripping over his own two feet. So we
agreed we would stick together. I only let him out of my sight once,
when he went to get his stupid Snapple."

Willy suddenly sobbed again, even more violently than before.

"We don't have a lot of time," Jim said.

Leia swatted him away. "Tell us what happened next," she said.
"Your friend went to get a Snapple. Then what?"

Willy extracted a tissue from his pocket, blew his nose, then put
it back in his pocket.

"He didn't come back," he said.

"Didn't come back from where?" Leia said.

"From the vending machines. Olson went with him to buy some
pretzels, and he saw the whole thing. Somehow the bottle got stuck
in the machine. Olson was rocking it back and forth while Carlisle was
trying to fish out the bottle. Somehow the whole thing tipped over
and crushed his skull."

"You're kidding," Jim said. "That's impossible."

"It's the curse," Willy insisted. "We tried to call the front desk,
tried to call 911. All we got were recordings or static. Finally Henderoff decided to go down to the lobby to get help. Olson and I stayed
behind."

"And I'm guessing Henderoff never came back, right?" Leia said.

"Right. Olson and I couldn't decide what to do next. We were
just sitting here scarfing down pretzels. Olson swallowed maybe two
handfuls when he choked and turned blue. I tried to save him. Really,
I did. But . . . "

"He choked on a pretzel?" Jim asked.

Willy shook his head. "Anaphylactic shock," he explained.

"Olson was violently allergic to peanuts."

"But you said he was eating *pretzels*," Leia said.

"He was eating pretzels that were manufactured in a factory that also processes peanuts. I looked at the bag afterward. There was a warning under the ingredients, but I guess Olson didn't notice it."

"There you have it," Jim said, as if the entire story made perfect sense. It didn't, really, but he didn't want to waste any more time babbling about Star Trek curses. Within the context of the day's events, there was no choice but to accept Willy's version of the events as fact. "Why don't you come downstairs with—"

"Excuse us just a minute," Leia interrupted firmly. "I need to talk to my friend in private."

She took Jim by the arm and guided him to the other side of the elevator landing.

"Were you *listening* to this guy?" Leia asked. "He's got goner written all over him. If we keep him around, we might get killed, too."

"You can't be serious. You make it sound like he's got cooties."

"*Death* cooties," Leia said. "Plus he's obviously in shock. If there's trouble he'll just curl up in the fetal position on the floor. I say we leave him right here."

She looked over her shoulder and waved pleasantly at Willy.

"And it's not like we're abandoning him," Leia continued. "He's probably got the best setup of anybody in this entire fleabag rattrap. There's enough candy bars and Diet Sprite in the minibars to keep him going for months. He could start his own civilization—provided he lives through the night."

Jim thought about it.

"You make a good point," he said. "But there's safety in numbers. Maybe I can motivate him to come with us."

"Good luck," Leia said. "I shot my motivational wad on the elevator, convincing you not to blow your head off."

They walked back to where Willy was waiting.

"This is the situation," Jim explained. "Cannibal zombies have overrun Houston and maybe the entire planet. This hotel is completely infested. We're trying to reach the seventh floor, where my sister and some of her friends are holed up. If the zombies bite you, you become one. Any questions?"

"No," Willy said, eyes wide with shock. "That's pretty much all I need to hear."

"But there's good news," Leia chimed in. "This floor, unlike the others, is zombie-free. And the zombies are too stupid to work doorknobs or use elevators. So as long as you stay put, you're safe. Safe from *them*, at least."

"Good, because I'm not going anywhere," Willy said. "I'll wait right here in room 1120 for whatever happens. With my luck, the ceiling will probably fall on my head."

Jim rolled his eyes.

"You need to come with us," he said. "You have no weapons and no training. You'd be a lot safer with me."

"I appreciate that," Willy said. "But if the ceiling's going to fall on my head, anyway, I'd feel better if I'm the only person it hits. No need to infect you guys with my goner cooties."

Leia's face pinked up. "Was I talking that loud?" she asked.

"Don't worry about it," Willy shrugged. "Safety first and all that. I'll walk with you guys to the door, but then you'll be free of me."

Together they stepped around the scaffolding and made their way toward the stairwell at the end of the hallway. Along the way, Leia gave voice to an idea. "We were looking for shoes when we found you," she said. "Maybe your friends have something I could borrow."

Willy looked down at her feet. "What size do you wear?"

"I don't know men's sizes. Something medium-ish."

"You mean like a seven or an eight?"

Again she blushed. "A man's size ten," she said.

"Seriously?" Jim blurted out.

Leia shot him a look.

Willy frowned. "You'd probably have to get those at a special store, like my mom does," he said. "She's got chronic edema."

"Now *there's* a plan," Leia said icily. "Once we're out of here I'll find a special store that sells gigantic shoes for my hideous, misshapen feet. Why didn't *I* think of that?"

She stalked off down the hallway.

Jim waved good-bye to Willy. "Stay put."

"I'd wish you good luck," Willy told him, "but I don't think I have any to give."

Leia was already at the stairwell door when Jim caught up with her. He opened it a crack and looked around. Satisfied that it was empty, he closed it again. All without saying a word.

"Why the silent treatment?" Leia asked him. "You can't possibly be mad. I'm the one who got called out over my clown feet."

"I'm not mad," Jim said. "I'm thinking. What you said about Willy staying here was right. This place is zombie-free. There's food. We could hole up here for a few hours until we determine a better plan."

"Brilliant," Leia said. "So we go downstairs and retrieve your friends?"

"How about *I* go retrieve my friends while you stay here?"

"Screw that," Leia said.

"Hear me out," Jim said. "It's a straight, zombie-free shot to seven. Once I reach the landing on their floor, I'll use my walkie-talkie to coordinate with the guys in Matt's suite. When they say the coast is clear, I'll run to their room. Then we'll reverse the procedure and bring everyone back here. It's idiot-proof."

Leia started to reply, then thought better of it. Instead, she felt around on her ammunition belt until she located Dexter's walkie-talkie. She switched it on.

"Dead Meat One, this is Dead Meat Two, do you read?" she said.

"This is Dead Meat One," came the reply. "Oh my God, is this the princess?"

"Gary?"

"Yeah. Are you all right? Is everything okay?"

"I'm fine."

"I'm fine, too," Jim added. "Thanks for asking."

"We're on the eleventh floor, about to take the stairs down to seven," Leia said. "But first we need you to tell us something: how far is the fire-exit door from your suite?"

"There's a fire-exit door?" Gary said.

Leia looked at Jim.

"How much of the hallway can you see from your room's peep-hole? Do you have any idea how many zombies are out there?"

"There's a lot of them," Gary said. "Pretty much all of them."

"Well, keep somebody at the door, because we're going to make our play pretty soon."

She switched off the radio.

"Your point?" Jim asked.

"My point is that you don't have any idea what's lurking on the stairs or waiting in that hallway. You need me."

"I need you someplace safe," Jim said.

"Dude, I'm not your girlfriend," Leia laughed. "You can skip the knight-in-shining-armor routine. Let's stay together and watch each other's backs. Besides, no place is safe. Ask Carlisle."

For the first time it registered to Jim that he was standing next to the vending area. He spotted, through its doorway, the bottom half of the unlucky red shirt's legs protruding from beneath the soda machine.

"Suit yourself," Jim said.

He drew his Taser, pushed open the fire-escape door, looked around again, and stepped inside. He held it for Leia. He was about to close it when he noticed Willy running down the hall toward them, a paper shopping bag in his hand.

"Wait!" he shouted.

Jim held the door. Willy ran up to them, panting.

"For the princess," he said, holding out the bag.

Leia stepped back into the hallway and looked at the package suspiciously, as if it might contain a bomb.

"For your feet," Willy said. "I'm sorry I didn't remember these sooner."

Willy set his grocery bag down and opened it. He withdrew what looked like an enormous plush model of the USS *Enterprise*— and then a second plush model shaped exactly like the first.

"What are those?" Leia asked.

"Slippers," Willy explained. "It's officially licensed merchandise. I got them at a con in Austin. They're way too big for me. But they're comfortable and they've got grippy stuff on the bottom, so you won't slip."

Leia looked at Willy, then at the shoes. Then back at Willy. She stepped forward, took the slippers, tossed them on the floor, and pushed her feet into them.

They went in quickly and easily.

"Cushy. Good fit," Leia said as she walked around experimentally. "And the grippers on the bottom work great."

"What do you think?" she asked Jim.

The sight of a six-foot-tall, nearly naked woman walking around in puffy novelty slippers as big as shoeboxes made him think a lot of things.

Things he wisely kept to himself.

"Great," he said. "Fantastic."

"I'll get these back to you," Leia promised Willy as she stepped into the stairwell.

"Don't worry about it," he replied. "I doubt I'll live long enough to wear them."

CHAPTER

15

WHAT ARE LITTLE GIRLS MADE OF?

The fire escape stairs were metal and the landings at each floor were composed of rough, unfinished concrete. To get from one level to the next, they had to descend a flight of stairs, turn around on a landing, and then descend another flight to a fire-escape door.

"Watch every turn," Jim whispered. "Listen for footsteps."

"I thought they couldn't do stairs," Leia whispered back.

"We don't *know* that. We're only guessing. Also, maybe one of the fire-escape doors is jammed open. There could be a dozen of those things milling around on one of the landings."

"And then what?"

Jim thought about it. He didn't have a clue.

"Let's hope there's not," he said.

They moved quietly, slowly making their way to the tenth floor. Leia was about to start down toward the ninth when Jim motioned for her to stop.

"I hear something," he said, pointing down.

The two of them stood motionless, listening, for what felt like an eternity.

"I hear it, too," Leia said. "Barely."

Jim stealthily descended the first flight of stairs to the switch-back, then gazed down the second flight. He saw the back of what he took to be a smallish woman, sitting on a step roughly halfway to the ninth-floor landing. Draped around her shoulders was an oversized man's jacket.

Leia followed close behind. "Zombie?" she whispered.

"No," Jim said. "Zombies don't cry."

Jim holstered his Taser, walked to the woman's side, and touched her shoulder. She looked up at him with a tear-streaked face. At once Jim recognized her clunky rectangular glasses and pointy prosthetic ears.

"Oh, my God," Jim said. "T'Poc?"

"Jim," she said. "What are you doing here?"

"We're trying to get to Matt's suite," Jim said.

T'Poc took off her glasses and wiped the right lens with the sleeve of her jacket. The left lens was shattered.

"So was I," she said as she put the glasses back on. "Didn't make it."

"Rayna told us you were dead," Jim said. "What happened?"

"You were right about the zombies. You tried to warn us and we just laughed at you."

"Never mind that," Jim said. "Tell me how you got up here."

"After the Klingon Feast, Matt wanted to go back to his suite, so we rode up to the seventh floor. When the elevator doors opened, we couldn't believe what we were seeing. We thought it was a prank. Some kind of GulfCon event. The blood was everywhere—on the walls, on the ceiling. There were people behind us in the elevator, pushing us out. We had to run past the feeding frenzy. We went right down the hallway toward Matt's room. Gary was first, then Rayna, then me, then Matt. There were lots of open doors, and the things in the rooms heard us, and they lunged as we passed. I dodged almost all of them. But then one of them grabbed my ankle. A real shoestring tackle. I fell flat on my face. Matt just leapt over me and kept on running."

"Were you bitten?" Jim asked.

"Of course I was. I had three or four zombies on top of me."

"And Matt didn't help at all?"

"He didn't even look back. By the time I kicked the creatures off me, he had the door to his suite already locked. So I kept running to the stairwell, and that's where I met the others. I was tempted to call them survivors, but that's not really the right word for these people. They were bitten, all of them, just hiding out and waiting to turn. One of them gave me his jacket to wear. They're nice . . . but they won't stay nice for long."

Jim listened carefully. He didn't hear any sounds coming from beneath them in the stairwell. "Where are they?"

"Two floors down," T'Poc said. "If you hurry, maybe you can still help them."

Jim was doubtful, but he tried to sound positive. "Sure, I'll ask about their stay. Make sure they have everything they need. See if they're interested in our turn-down service." He winked at Leia. "Be right back."

The two women watched him descend the stairs, then looked to each other.

"What's that perfume you're wearing?" T'Poc said.

"Excuse me?" Leia asked.

"Your perfume. It's great."

"I'm not wearing anything," Leia said. "Except a metal bikini that chafes whenever I run too fast."

"It's a pretty awesome costume. I'm not loving the shoes, but I'll give you big props for showing serious skin. You've got beautiful arms. Really well-shaped muscle definition. So why not flaunt it, right? I'm a big believer in giving the people what they want. As long as the convention center isn't freezing."

"I know exactly what you mean," Leia said.

"I had a friend who had the opposite problem. She used to dress as an Orion slave girl. If she got even a little bit warm, she sweated. And every time she sweated, the paint came off. One time, at a show in Baton Rouge, the con made her pay for a hotel chair she ruined."

"Green paint is a bitch," Leia said. "I try not to wear it any longer than I have to."

"Take a look at my costume this time," T'Poc said.

With a great deal of effort she stood up, then let the jacket drop from her shoulders.

"Oh, my God," Leia said. She took a step backward.

"Awesome, isn't it?" T'Poc said. "It's the two-piece crew uniform from 'Mirror, Mirror,' the episode where Kirk and the rest of the bridge crew are transported to an alternate universe where barbarians rule and the female crewmembers dress like NBA cheerleaders. The only drawback is that I had to do crunches for weeks just to get in shape."

Leia didn't respond. She was too busy looking at the two deep, ragged bites on T'Poc's stomach.

"Those don't hurt," T'Poc said, following her gaze. "Not anymore. At first it was so bad I thought I was going to die. But after a while it got better."

Leia kept staring at the wounds. They definitely weren't getting better. They wept blood. And the skin ringing them was greenish gray. Like a corpse.

"I guess that's why I'm still hanging on. I thought I could beat the odds. But I don't think I will. I'm weak as hell, and I'm having all sorts of strange thoughts and urges. Especially the hunger. I'm ravenous. I don't know how much longer I can control it. I mean . . . right now we're having a normal conversation, but I really just want to bite one of your delicious-looking biceps. Do you do Pilates?"

"Hatha yoga," Leia said as she took a step back. "Also free weights. It's the best way to stay toned."

She pulled her Taser.

"I'm going to check on Jim," she said. "Don't you move an inch."

She started down the stairs.

"Wait," T'Poc said. "I have to tell you one last thing. It's important."

Leia hesitated.

"I've started hearing things in my head. They tell me to do stuff. But they also tell me . . . how this is all going to end."

"How?" Leia said.

"We're all going to die, Princess. You, Jim, me, every last one of us. Everywhere."

A moan wafted up the stairwell. Then another—followed by the unmistakable mayhem of a struggle. And then Leia, swearing under her breath, launched herself down the steps toward the sounds of slaughter.

CHAPTER

16

AMOK TIME

Jim quietly descended the stairs until he stood halfway down the last flight before the seventh-floor landing. He knelt and peered over the rail. What he saw turned his stomach.

The pack of decrepit figures below him weren't waiting to become zombies as T'Poc had suggested; their transformation was already complete. Jim counted six, all crowded in a half-circle, dressed in colorful alien costumes and hunched over an unmoving body dressed in a blue uniform from the original series.

The three zombies in front, women in shiny dresses and thigh-high silver boots, crouched low over the body's head. *What are they doing?* Jim thought, then immediately wished he could un-ask the question as all three women rose unsteadily, all struggling to wrest possession of the corpse's naked, bloody brain. Jim didn't know whether the wave of horror coursing through his stomach came from the unspeakable sight itself—or from his sickening realization that its perpetrators were dressed as the alien organ thieves from the episode "Spock's Brain" and that their zombified remnants had kicked the role-play up a notch.

He knew he should just Taser them. Stand there on the steps, just out of reach, and zap them like a firing squad. It was a rational, low-risk plan.

But as Jim watched two of the undead horrors claw through the ersatz Vulcan's shirt and abdomen and begin quarreling over a length of large intestine, he felt rationality take a backseat to rage. Tasering was too easy for these monsters. They needed to suffer.

One of the creatures, dressed as some sort of reptilian alien soldier, turned its back to him. Slung across its back was what looked like a stainless-steel, art-deco-style ax with a long blade and a pointed tip. Unlike the smooth-edged blades that Martock was selling on the convention floor, this one appeared to be razor-sharp and in complete violation of GulfCon rules and regulations.

Another plan, one far less rational, jelled in his mind. Jim knew he could do a lot of damage very quickly with that weapon. Then he wouldn't have to waste a bunch of Taser darts. This seemed like a perfectly reasonable strategy—or as reasonable as he could manage with the sound of his every heartbeat echoing through his ears.

And there was no one around—not Rayna, not Leia—to tell him any different.

He stood, walked quickly and quietly down the last steps, crossed the floor to the scene of the slaughter, and then ripped the weapon off the soldier zombie's back. The creature turned, its third eye fixed on the last thing it would ever see: Jim slamming the blade down onto the center of its host's skull, splitting it like a melon.

One down.

The other zombies, finally alerted to his presence, moaned and tottered around to face him. Jim didn't give them time to get their bearings. He rocked the ax free of its former owner and then used it to sweep a fat Ferengi's feet out from under him. The blade's impact severed the zombie's right leg just below the knee. The monster fell face-first on the concrete—still moving, but crippled.

Two down.

The trio of zombies in the shiny dresses fumbled and dropped the Vulcan's brain; it landed on the floor with a wet splat. Against Jim's will, a short, hysterical laugh escaped his lips.

"You like brains?" he yelled as he swung viciously, severing one creature's head with a single stroke. "Who wants some more?" He reversed his grip, swung backhanded, and decapitated another. The third watched in confusion as the two heads landed at her feet, followed by the rest of their bodies. Then it looked back at Jim, its dead eyes caked in '60s-era go-go eye shadow.

He again bit down on his revulsion and swung one more right-handed arc—and then there were three headless corpses crumpled in a heap. *Hat trick!* Jim thought, feeling a grin spread across his face.

He was breathing hard. His arms burned from the exertion. And there was still one more zombie to go, the one at the rear of the pack that was keeping its back to him. It appeared to be a middle-aged man with gray, shoulder-length hair. His costume looked like it was sewn from rags. On his left hand was a glove that appeared slightly familiar.

"Who the hell are *you* supposed to be?" Jim asked, grabbing it by the shoulder and spinning it around.

The zombie moaned and staggered toward him.

Suddenly Jim's face brightened. He remembered.

"Khan!" he shouted as he pointed his ax at the undead horror. "Khaaannnn!"

He was raising his weapon to strike when the creature suddenly stopped in its tracks, twitched like a marionette, then went slack and fell to the floor. Behind it stood Leia, Taser in hand. The thin wires that had channeled fifty thousand volts into the zombie's back trailed from it to her weapon.

"Thanks," Jim said. "How long were you standing there?"

"Long enough to fully appreciate what an idiot you are," she said. "Are you out of your tiny, twenty-watt mind? You could have done all this with a Taser."

"This was a lot more satisfying," Jim said, still breathing heavily.

"And borderline suicidal," Leia said. "Come here."

Jim dropped his blood-swathed weapon on the floor and walked to the princess, who stood at the base of the stairs.

Leia performed a careful, walk-around inspection of him. Lastly, she took his hands into hers. She closely examined each digit, then ran her fingers lightly over his palms, looking for the smallest cut. She found nothing. She looked up to find Jim watching her intently.

"You're okay," she said, meeting his gaze.

"That was just an excuse to feel me up," he said, smiling.

"Don't get cute. What you did was idiotic. And you didn't just risk your own life. One bite and you're lost to us. Lost to your sister, lost to me. Think about that before you play hero again."

"Heroism had nothing to do with it," Jim said sullenly.

He heard a moan behind him. He turned to see the one-legged Ferengi, still facedown on the concrete, slowly crawling toward them.

"Excuse me," he said.

He picked up his weapon, walked to the creature, flipped it over with his boot, and drove the corner of the ax blade into its third eye. Then he shouldered the weapon and walked back to Leia.

"I'm not a hero," Jim said. "I just lost my mind a little. Because—well, because I saw Mr. Spock lose his."

Jim motioned toward the mostly eaten corpse on the floor.

Then he noticed that Leia was already staring at it. And that her left hand gripped the stair rail so hard her knuckles were white.

"It moved," she whispered. "Just a twitch, but I saw it."

Jim walked slowly back to the body. It lay in the middle of a gooey mass of blood and gore. Its entire belly had been wrenched open. Bits of blue and pink organ meat lay strewn about. What remained of the head was better left unexamined.

"Are you sure?" he asked.

Just then the right leg twitched again. A moment later the left arm did the same.

"It isn't possible," Leia said as she walked cautiously to his side. "There's nothing left."

"Look," Jim said, pointing.

As they watched, a small white nodule sprouted just underneath the corpse's exposed left collarbone. It expanded with startling speed. As it grew it sent long, white, spaghetti-thin tendrils snaking throughout the body. Several vined around the spine. Others raced down the ruined limbs. A bundle of them forced their way through the neck and began grasping about for pieces of skull to gather.

"I think I may get sick," Leia said.

Jim didn't reply. He was too busy watching the transformation of a human corpse into a zombie.

The nodule expanded to the size of an orange, then stopped. A horizontal crease formed on its surface. A moment later the crease split open, revealing a glaring red eye.

"It's taken over the body," Jim said. "But it's in for a surprise."

The invader tried to work the newborn zombie's limbs. Leia and Jim watched as first one, then the other arm shuddered. But that was all the parasite could manage. Too many muscles were gone, too many tendons, for real movement. The severely damaged body was of no use to its new owner.

Jim knelt down beside the corpse and stared at the eye.

"I guess it sucks to be you, huh, Twitchy?" he said.

The eye stared back at him. Jim wondered where it came from. Whether it felt malice or fear or rage over its predicament—or anything at all.

He leaned closer to get a better look.

Then, closer still.

He felt an almost primal urge, welling up from deep inside his subconscious, to touch it.

Leia grabbed his jacket and pulled him back.

"What the hell were you doing?" she shouted. "You were leaning right into the damn thing."

Jim shook his head to clear the cobwebs.

"That was close," he said, nodding. "You don't want to hold eye contact for very long. They can get inside your head. That's probably what happened to Janice. They screwed with her mind and made her open the hotel doors."

"Kill it," Leia said.

"In a second."

Jim plucked the can of Mace from Leia's gun belt.

"Why do you want that?" she asked.

"Another experiment."

He pointed the Mace at the eye and fired a stream of caustic fluid into it. The reaction was everything he'd hoped for. The corpse that the creature controlled jerked spasmodically—exactly the way a body would react if its master were in agony.

"Finish it," Leia said.

"Why the rush?" Jim asked. "Feeling softhearted?"

"We've got things to do. Remember T'Poc? She's still up there."

"I know," Jim said. "Believe me, I know."

He stood up, put the Mace canister back into Leia's belt, and then brought up his ax.

He was about to use it when the princess took the weapon from him. She leaned over the corpse and gouged out the eyeball herself.

"*That's* how softhearted I am," she said.

She stared at the mass of biological wreckage that had once been a person. Jim silently held out his hand for the blade. Leia lifted it—and, growling deep in her throat, thrust its sharp point back into the monstrosity three more times.

"And stay down!" she spat at the thing.

Then she handed the weapon back to Jim.

CHAPTER

17

THE FIRST DUTY

"You made it,"T'Poc said when they rounded the switchback in front of her. The look of relief on her face seemed genuine.

"I did," Jim said. "But you knew they were already dead when you sent me down there, didn't you?"

A tear traced down T'Poc's left cheek.

"Yes," she replied quietly. "Half an hour ago, some guy came running up for help from one of the lower floors and they grabbed him. I heard everything. They took forever to finish him."

"Why did you send Jim down there?" Leia asked.

"I couldn't help it. I knew it wasn't safe. I knew it. But they wouldn't let me warn you."

"Who?" Leia said.

"Whatever's inside me. Whatever got into my blood when that zombie prick bit me. I'm getting smaller and they're getting bigger, and it won't be long until I'm gone. Just talking to you is taking . . . everything that's left of me."

T'Poc pulled down the corner of her top, revealing a bulge near her right collarbone. It moved around fitfully, as if desperately seeking a way out.

"Think I should have this looked at?" she said.

Jim laughed. It sounded bitter and unhealthy.

He walked up the stairs to T'Poc, sat down beside her, and stared up at Leia.

"I need you to go down to the next flight and stay there," he said. "I'll catch up in a minute."

"You're serious?" Leia asked. "You think I can't handle this?"

"I'm not asking for you," he said. "I'm asking for me."

Leia reluctantly descended the stairs, glancing once over her shoulder. T'Poc and Jim sat silently until she was out of sight.

"I really don't want to come back," T'Poc said. "I think it would be lame."

"Exceedingly lame," Jim said.

"I'm sorry you have to do this."

"Not as sorry as me."

"I'd kill for a cigarette right now."

"That won't be necessary."

Jim pulled a crushed, well-worn pack from his back pocket, fished out a smoke, and handed it to her. Then he produced a book of hotel matches and struck one.

T'Poc lit up and took a long drag. For a moment she seemed to regain a little bit of color, a little bit of her old self.

But only for a moment.

"Did you know we were going to hook up this weekend? I decided right after we met in the parking garage. Guess that's out of the question now. Maybe next month at Dragon*Con."

"I'll mark my calendar," Jim said.

He stood up, walked up two steps behind where T'Poc sat, pulled off his backpack and rummaged through it.

"You need to get Gary and Rayna away from Matt," T'Poc said, staring straight ahead. "You can't trust him."

"I'm working on it."

Jim pulled out the Glock, clicked off the safety, and chambered a round.

She didn't turn around. "Is that a gun?"

"This won't hurt," he said.

"How would you know?" T'Poc asked.

She took one more drag on the cigarette and then stubbed it out on the stair.

Jim pointed the pistol at the back of T'Poc's skull. Just before he squeezed the trigger, she spoke one last time—in a strange, empty voice that was part her, part something else. Something that was trying very hard to stop her.

"These things . . . the things that make the zombies . . . they aren't from around here," she said. "They don't have thoughts, but I see images . . . pictures of darkness and emptiness and cold. They came here from someplace far away. They made the dead rise. But the zombies aren't your only problem. There's something else. I can sense it out there. It's a thousand times worse than the undead or the things that made them. Because it still has its mind. And Matt . . . "

"What?" Jim said. "Tell me now, before it's too late."

"There's something wrong with him, Jim. He's worse than crazy. He has . . . a connection . . . There is a network . . . "

T'Poc's voice stopped suddenly, as if someone grabbed her by the throat. She slumped against the stair rail, lifeless.

A moment passed. Then another.

She sat up again and turned to face Jim. The bulge on her shoulder split open as he watched, revealing a pulsating eye.

The eye locked on Jim. The thing that had been T'Poc let out a moan.

Jim pointed the Glock and fired a round directly into the big red pupil. It exploded in a spray of greenish slime.

And may God have mercy on my soul, he thought.

18

WRONGS DARKER THAN DEATH OR NIGHT

Leia walked all the way back to the section of stairs just above the seventh-floor landing. She sat at the top so that she couldn't see or smell the charnel house below.

She tried to prepare herself for the sound of the bullet. But she still jumped when the Glock's sharp report echoed off the stairwell's cold, blank walls.

Not long afterward Jim descended the stairs, the pistol still in his hand.

"We have to get out of here," he said. "T'Poc started to warn me about Matt. She's not sure what's wrong with him, but I don't want the guy anywhere near my sister."

"Fine, but how do we get past *them*?" Leia said.

She pointed in the direction of the landing door. It rattled under the blows of the zombies on the other side.

"Why are they so riled?" Jim asked.

"The noise from your one-man battle brought them all down here. Maybe you can dream up a way to get rid of them."

Jim walked to the bottom of the stairs, recovered the ax, and trudged back to Leia. He sat down beside her, the gore-covered weapon at his feet.

He put his head in his hands. He felt unspeakably tired. Not for the first time, he wished for some help. The killing and the running were easy. He and Leia could take care of that themselves. But to what end? Was there any way out of this mess? He wished he were smarter, wished he had access to someone like Dr. Sandoval, the exobiologist from Harvard. Maybe he knew of some weakness in the zombies that could be exploited.

But that was nuts.

Still thinking like a Trekkie, Jim thought grimly. *Still looking for a silver bullet to settle the problem before the credits roll. Sandoval is almost definitely dead by now. And an ivory-tower egghead wouldn't help much, anyway. He'd just slow us down.*

"Are you okay?" Leia asked, jolting him out of his reverie.

"I'm trying to think of a plan."

A minute crawled by.

Finally, she asked, "Is this just a ploy to get me alone?"

Jim forced a weary smile.

"I *am* glad you're here," he said. "Gladder than you probably know. How are you feeling?"

"I'm maintaining. Why?"

"It's always rough the first time," he said. "Your first kill."

"Who said it was my first?"

Jim's surprised expression made Leia smile.

"I'm kidding. Besides, I don't think these count as real kills. How can you kill something that's already dead?"

"Good point," Jim said.

"And I've got a hunch this isn't *your* first time," Leia said. "How are *you* holding up?"

Jim took a deep breath, as if he were about to speak at length. Then, at the last moment, he seemed to change his mind.

"Army snipers have an old saying," he offered instead. "The only thing I feel when I pull the trigger is recoil."

"I take it you're not very big on sharing."

"Trust me, you can't grasp the stuff that happened over there unless you lived it. Until you've actually been in battle and seen people die in front of you . . . "

His words trailed off in midsentence. He looked into Leia's eyes.

"Under the current circumstances, I guess that sounds stupid," he said.

"Yes," Leia answered. "But I'll forgive the oversight if you answer one simple question: How do you go from working as a first-rate soldier to working in a third-rate hotel?"

"It's easy," Jim sighed. "First you join the army right out of high school and pull two tours in Afghanistan—the second as a platoon squad leader. You win a Purple Heart and a Bronze Star, big freaking deal, but soon the responsibility gives you insomnia. Because in spite of the medals and the uniform, you're just twenty years old and you still don't know shit. And maybe, the night before a raid, you start puking blood and they put you in the infirmary. And while you're lying on your back instead of walking in the field with your troop, your squad goes into a booby-trapped house, two guys die, and one guy loses his sight. And when this news gets back to the infirmary, you *know* you could have prevented it. You *know* you would have smelled the trouble and avoided it. But you *weren't* there, because you were laid up with what turns out to be a pansy-ass bleeding ulcer. A stress-induced stomach lesion brought on by your fear that you might let your people down. Talk about irony."

Jim tapped the end of the ax handle on the floor.

"So I finished my hitch and got out. I didn't want any more re-sponsibility. I wanted a bullshit civilian job where I was free to screw up without consequences. Which the Botany Bay offered me. Until tonight, at least."

"Tonight, everything changes," Leia agreed. "They'll be rewrit-ing the history books after this one. Assuming we survive long enough to need them."

"Now I've got a question for you," Jim said. "What compels a smart, attractive young woman to spend her weekends pretending that she's Carrie Fisher in what is arguably the worst film of the original *Star Wars* trilogy?"

Leia laughed. "You want the short answer or the long answer?"

Jim glanced at the fire door. It shook from the constant onslaught of zombies on the opposite side. "I'm in no real hurry to go out there," he said.

Leia pulled her legs up to her chest and wrapped her arms around them.

"Then I'm going to do something I rarely do," she said. "I'm going to confide in you. Normally, I keep this story to myself, but since we're likely to be eaten alive before midnight, I feel like I can share this with you."

"I appreciate that," Jim said.

Leia sighed, rocked back and forth on the step nervously, then began.

"I grew up near Amarillo. I was a pretty normal kid until I turned eleven. That's when my father decided to leave my mother and me. You know that Springsteen song, 'Hungry Heart'?"

"'I went out for a ride and I never went back.'"

"Bingo. Dad went off to work one day and didn't come home

that evening. Can you imagine? I thought he was dead. Then we got a postcard a few weeks later from San Diego saying he was done with us. He actually wrote 'done with us.' I can recite the entire message if you'd like."

"Why did he leave?"

"I was a kid. I figured it was my fault. And when I finally screwed up the courage to ask my mom, I learned that I was right."

"How?"

"I wasn't actually his kid. My biological father shacked up with my mom for a one-night stand. My pretend father found out and split. I guess he didn't want a pretend daughter. Which is too bad, because the pretend daughter really liked him. Loved him, I guess."

"What did you do?"

"What could I do? I toughed it out. Mom married a new asshole, and this one abused her. She wouldn't leave him. So one night at the dinner table, I put a steak knife through his hand. The paramedics had to pry it out of the table. That worked out well, actually. They sent me to a boarding school two hundred miles away. After that I went to Ohio State and graduated premed. And that's how I wound up here at GulfCon in a Princess Leia costume."

"Wait, go back a minute," Jim said. "I think I missed something."

"Like I said, I graduated premed. Most of my regular college bills were covered by scholarships. But if I'm going to do medical school, I need some serious bank. So last summer I answered this ad from a video game company. They needed a model to wear shorts and a sports bra and carry a big fake gun at a convention. That was the day I discovered my calling. Now I do these things almost every weekend."

"Is that how you got into science fiction?"

"No, I came by that naturally. Other worlds are better than this one, you know?"

"I do," Jim sighed. "I used to watch *Star Trek* and dream about being on the *Enterprise*, half a galaxy away from my mom, from our poor-ass existence, from pretty much everything."

"Same here," Leia said. "Only I fantasized about being half a galaxy away from my mother and stepfather, surrounded by people who really were decent and honorable, and not just pretending. People I could count on in a jam."

"We're a match made in heaven. No wonder you didn't want to stay behind on the eleventh floor. You thought I'd ditch you."

A peculiar look crossed Leia's face.

"Actually, no," she said. "I never thought you were going to ditch me. I just figured my chances are better with you than with the last surviving member of the West Texas Red Tunic Club."

A hideous moan from the hallway interrupted their discussion.

"Though it doesn't change the fact that we're trapped in this stairwell," Leia said.

Jim's face suddenly brightened.

"We're not trapped at all," he said. "I just figured out what to do."

"You see?" Leia said. "I knew you wouldn't let me down."

19

MOVE ALONG HOME

Jim took out his walkie-talkie and toggled it on.

"Gary, this is Jim," he said. "Come back."

"Where the hell are you?" Gary responded. "We thought we heard a gunshot. Is the princess safe?"

"She's fine. Where's Matt?"

"He's holed up in the bedroom. And still acting really strange."

"In what way?"

"I don't know if I can explain it. But he hasn't made one fat joke since we left the feast. No more cracks about my mom. And he's stopped eyeballing your sister's ass. It's really disconcerting."

Jim tried not to let the remark distract him from the plan. "Don't disturb him," he said. "I'll deal with Matt later, but right now we need your help. Can you go over to the atrium window?"

"I'm standing there right now," Gary said. "Where are you?"

"We're in the east fire stairwell on the seventh floor. There's about a million zombies standing between us and you. We need something to draw them off. I want you to check the four atrium elevators. Where are they?"

"One's down in the lobby," Gary said. "Plus one on the second floor and one on what looks like the fifteenth floor. They're all full of zombies. But the one you rode to eleven is still empty."

"Like I figured," Jim said. "Now here's where it gets tricky. Do the room phones still work?"

"Yeah," Gary said.

"Excellent. I want you to contact a guy named Willy in room 1120. Tell him to go to the elevators and push the call button. The one on the eleventh floor should open right up. I need him to send that elevator to the seventh floor and then hop back out, understand?"

"Got it."

"Once you're finished, call me. We want to be ready to move when the elevator arrives. Hopefully it will make a nice, loud ding, which the zombies will mistake for a dinner bell. Then we'll sneak down to you."

"Genius," Gary said.

"Make it so," Jim replied.

He clicked off the walkie-talkie.

"You have your moments," Leia said. "Not many of them, but you do have them."

Jim sighed, closed his eyes, and rubbed his temple. "*Empire Strikes Back*," he said.

"What?"

"That's a line from—"

The walkie-talkie crackled to life, cutting him off.

"Jim, it's Rayna," the voice said. "I just got off the phone with your new buddy, Willy. He's going to the elevator now."

"Perfect," Jim said. "We're ready to move."

"But he wants you to wait for him."

"What?"

"He said he's changed his mind about staying behind. He wants to join us. He's going to send the elevator, then run down the fire-escape stairs and connect with you."

Jim swore under his breath.

"He better run fast. We'll give him one minute, but that's it."

"Listen for the ding," Rayna told him. "The elevator's moving. Tenth floor, ninth floor . . . "

Jim stood up and shouldered his ax. Leia got up, too. They walked down to the landing and picked their way past the bloody corpses to the fire door.

"Eighth floor," Rayna said.

Above his head, Jim heard a door to the stairwell open. Ensign Willy was on the move.

"Seventh floor," Rayna said.

Jim put his head to the door and heard a faint, distant *ding*.

"Suppertime," Rayna said. "It's hard to tell for sure, but I think they're going for it."

"See you soon," Jim said, clicking off.

Moments later, a completely winded Willy clambered down the stairs.

"Welcome to the party," Leia said.

Willy waved halfheartedly, then doubled over and put his hands on his knees. He stayed that way through breath after ragged breath.

"We have to go," Jim said.

Willy held up one finger. Then he took several more breaths. Then he stood up, his face still beet red. His eyes landed on Jim's weapon.

"Nice kar'takin," he said between gasps.

"Huh?" Jim replied.

"Your ax," Willy said. "It's the primary melee weapon of the Jem'Hadar shock troops of the Dominion. From *Deep Space Nine*."

"So that's what it's called," Jim said. "I didn't know. I guess I was never that big of a Niner."

Willy inspected the blade more closely.

"Ugh," he said. "It's got zombie stuff all over it."

"It'll be worse in a minute," Jim said, then pushed open the door.

The zombies, the nearest of which were perhaps twenty yards away and stumbling farther down the hall toward the elevator, didn't notice.

Suddenly Leia grabbed Jim's face and kissed him. For half an instant, there were no zombies, no horrors, just soft lips and an effortless sense of togetherness. Then she pulled back and they both drew a breath.

"For luck," she said.

"That's from . . . never mind. Here we go."

They started their careful, cautious journey down the hall.

20

THE CHANGELING

Matt lay motionless in the darkness, sprawled across his hotel bed. He was so exhausted when he lay down that he hadn't bothered to pull back the bedspread.

He'd stayed there for what seemed like days. He was tired, but he never slept. Not for a moment. Instead, he listened to the sounds outside his door. This was remarkably easy. His hearing had grown superhumanly acute. When Rayna asked Gary if there was any bottled water in the minibar, he heard it. When some sort of melee erupted down the hall, he heard it.

And just moments ago, when Jim announced over the walkie-talkie that he was standing at the door of the seventh-floor fire escape, waiting for just the right moment to rush down to the suite, he heard that, too.

The news made Matt very, very upset.

I run a tight ship, he thought. *I won't have some insubordinate, shoe-shining, room-service-tray-fetching primate undermining my authority.*

He quietly sat up and lowered his feet to the floor. He looked around. His vision was so sharp that the pitch-black room didn't seem all that dark anymore. His sensitive eyes observed its every feature.

Perhaps they were a touch *too* sensitive. The sliver of light seeping under the door was too painful to look at.

Matt reached over to the nightstand, where he had deposited his trusty Ray-Bans before lying down. He put them on.

Better. Much better.

He felt like a new man.

Pain and fear had forced his retreat into darkness and quiet. Rayna and Gary's loud, ceaseless prattling drove him to distraction. So did the suite's insanely bright lights. He had to escape to a quiet, dark place to sort things out. To process what was happening to him.

It had begun shortly after he reached the suite. He, Rayna, and Gary got there by running a gauntlet of the undead. One of them attacked him. Instinctively he punched it in the face, knocking it to the floor. Then he stomped on its head.

He kept racing down the hall, right over T'Poc. She'd fallen. One of the undead things was climbing on top of her, about to take its first bite. Not his problem. As he explained to Gary earlier in the day, man shouldn't interfere with nature's rhythms.

Once behind closed doors, they were okay. Yet for some reason Matt couldn't stop sweating. His skin crawled. His limbs ached.

Even worse, he felt a stirring deep inside his psyche. As if something had hitched a ride in his mind.

He went into the bathroom and splashed water on his face, trying to calm himself. Then he spotted a small, almost unnoticeable cut on one knuckle. It came, he guessed, from popping the zombie in the face.

He'd seen enough movies to know what such blood-to-blood contact could mean. He grew more and more agitated about it. Finally, he simply walked into the bedroom, closed the door, and cut himself off from the others.

Just as the urges in his head told him to.

At first he was frightened. He lay trembling in the dark, his clothes soaked with sweat. He couldn't close his eyes, for fear he'd awaken as a zombie. But slowly the fear eased. Slowly his discomfort lessened.

Slowly the things in his mind grew more powerful. And as their powers grew, they began to work wonders.

They improved his ears and eyes. They made his muscles stronger. They made his brain work faster. All stress and uncertainty receded.

This is way better than Xanax, Matt thought.

The only topic that tickled anything approaching discord was the news of Jim Pike's imminent arrival. That, and the obvious glee that his surviving crew, Gary and Rayna, displayed at the prospect.

This is textbook treason, he thought.

He knew their plans. How some kid upstairs helped distract the zombies. How they'd figured out that Tasers worked on the undead. Even how they'd met a wounded T'Poc on the stairs and discovered Matt's role in her demise.

He puzzled over that last bit of information. He couldn't remember how he knew it. Yet there it was, tucked away in his cerebral cortex, like some random bit of trivia he'd discovered while surfing the Web. *Where did I read that again? How do I know this?*

He also knew, somehow, that Jim was furious. That he wanted Matt's head on a stick.

The thought made him smile.

Matt stood up and walked to the bedroom door. Based on the sounds outside, he knew exactly where his suitemates were. Rayna stood at the door, waiting to admit her brother. Gary was right behind her, anxiously rocking back and forth, the soft friction of his sneakers creating a noise that was imperceptible to human ears but rang clear as a bell to Matt.

They were committing the vilest treason. Bringing visitors aboard, behind the commanding officer's back. Visitors who actually meant to do him harm.

Matt placed his hand on the doorknob. His body tensed for action.

Time for the big fight scene, he thought.

He opened the bedroom door and stepped out into the light.

CHAPTER

21

Insurrection

The hallway was littered with corpses of the freshly dead. Too fresh, Jim hoped, to rise quite yet, but there was no way to know for sure. Everything he'd seen suggested that the incubation period was wildly inconsistent: some people turned within minutes; others took several hours. Why?

He and Leia and Willy picked their way among the carnage, carefully watching for movement. It wasn't easy because, just as on the third floor, most of the light sconces had been destroyed. This was another puzzle. He'd already concluded that the zombies were too dumb to open doors—so how could they make the strategic decision to smash the lights one by one? The only possible explanation was that it *wasn't* a strategic decision—that the creatures were operating by base instinct. They did not like light. And now that the sun was down, they were coming out in force.

Jim glanced up to see Rayna, still wearing her electric-blue Andorian face paint, cautiously open the suite's door. She motioned for them to hurry. He motioned, just as emphatically, for her to stay inside until they got closer.

Something grabbed his left ankle.

Jim looked down to see the bloodied face of a man in his forties, his blue tunic pulled up to expose his prodigiously hairy paunch. A paunch that sprouted a bloodshot eyeball just above the belly button.

Jim shook his ankle free and then punctured the eye with the tip of his kar'takin.

Leia pointed down the hall to another freshly minted zombie—an elderly woman who doddered to her feet as they watched, then lurched toward them, toothless mouth agape.

As he advanced on his target, Jim briefly wondered what front-desk moron gave the old lady a room on the Trekkie floor. Then he realized she wore a ragged, bloodied *Next Gen* medical uniform.

Fandom knows no age limits, he thought.

He swung the kar'takin. The blow sliced off the top of the creature's fragile-looking skull, exposing a neat cross section of its brain. The body tumbled to the floor.

Jim surveyed the hall for other potential targets. He glanced back at the suite. His sister was still watching. She'd covered her mouth with her hand and seemed on the edge of fainting. She'd seen more carnage than she'd ever imagined, and things were going to get worse before they got better.

He glanced behind him, making sure Leia and Willy kept close. Then he looked back at the door.

Rayna wasn't there anymore.

In her place stood Matt. He was grinning.

"Sorry, Jim, but your sister and I would like a little privacy." He reached out and hung a Do Not Disturb sign from the door handle.

"Be quiet," Jim said. "They'll hear you."

"Hear me?" Matt shouted. *"You're worried that all the zombies down the hall are going to hear me? And maybe they're going to shamble down here and tear you to pieces?"*

Jim started running, but it was too late. Matt slammed the door in his face and the automatic lock clicked into place.

"What just happened?" Leia shouted. "What the hell is he doing?"

"Trying to kill us," Jim said. Some two dozen zombies had abandoned the elevators and were now shambling toward them.

Leia hammered on the door. "Let us in!" she shouted. "Please!"

Willy joined her. "Open the goddamn door!"

Jim looked at the peephole. He sensed that Matt was on the other side, watching them.

"We can't stay here," Leia said.

Jim handed his kar'takin to Leia, reached into his jacket, and pulled out a lanyard with a universal passkey attached. He passed it over the door's sensor pad. A tiny light near the knob changed from red to green. The locking mechanism clicked.

Jim turned the knob, put his shoulder against the door, and pushed.

It didn't budge.

"What's wrong now?" Willy asked nervously, his eyes locked on the advancing undead.

"Door must be barricaded," Jim said, straining against it.

Leia pushed, too. It didn't help.

"We don't have time for this," she said. "We've got to—"

She was cut off by a high-pitched shriek from Willy.

A corpse they'd just stepped over—a woman dressed in a miniskirt uniform from the original series—rose up, moaned, and stumbled toward them. Leia dispatched it with a sharp jab from the kar'takin, cleanly bisecting its third eye.

"We're out of time," she said.

Jim hit the door repeatedly with his shoulder.

Meanwhile, a solid wall of zombies, filling the hallway from side to side, shambled toward them.

"They're coming!" Willy shouted.

Jim tried to think of them only as a faceless swarm, a strategic obstacle, but little bits of lost humanity insisted on jumping out at him: a ridged Klingon forehead here, a torn Romulan tunic there. A scrolling LED lanyard that blinked: *Frak Me? Frak You!*

"We've got to get back to the stairwell!" Leia insisted.

"No," Jim said.

Instead, he retreated to the door of the adjacent room. He could hear scratching and moaning from the other side. Jim took out his passkey and turned to Leia.

"Tase this prick as soon as it steps out," he said.

Leia tossed the kar'takin to Willy and then pulled her Taser just as Jim unlocked the room, shoved open the door, and stepped back.

Out stumbled two bedraggled-looking zombies, the first wearing bloodied pajamas, the second a pair of boxer shorts. Leia tased the first as soon as it cleared the threshold. Jim grabbed the second by the shoulders, spun it in the direction of the other zombies, and sent it sailing toward them with a boot to the butt.

"Get in!" he shouted, pushing the others inside and slamming the door in the faces of the advancing horde.

"Now what?" Leia and Willy asked at the same time.

Jim didn't reply. Instead, he switched on the overhead light, tossed his backpack in a chair, pulled out the Glock, and chambered a round.

"Stay in here," Jim said. "Keep out of sight."

Through the wall he could hear Rayna's voice. She was crying and pleading. Begging Matt to unlock the door.

Jim located the interior door that linked the room to Matt's suite. Again he swiped his passkey, but this time he kicked the door open. The force of the blow nearly knocked it off its hinges.

Matt was standing near the exterior door, gripping Rayna's right arm by the wrist. Gary lay on the floor, groaning.

"Commodore Stockard, you are unfit for command," Jim said. "I'm here to relieve you of duty."

Then he aimed the Glock at Matt's face and advanced on him. This should have been enough to get the job done. Jim knew that nearly all civilians shrank away from the sight of a gun barrel. Especially if it was inches from their face. But Matt never flinched.

"This is *my* ship," he hissed.

"You're one of them," Jim concluded. "You're not human anymore."

"No," Matt said. "I'm better."

He released Rayna, then brought up his right arm with superhuman speed, batting the gun out of the way. Then he delivered a stunning head butt, knocking Jim off his feet. The Glock flew out of his hand, bounced across the floor, and stopped a foot short of the wide-open connecting door.

Jim's ears rang and his eyes blurred. When he finally regained his senses, he found Matt standing over him.

"You need to respect the chain of command," Matt said.

He walked over to the pistol, knelt down, and picked it up. He inspected it carefully.

"I don't really need this," he said, glancing back at Jim. "Not the way I am now. But I think I'll hold onto it just the same."

He was so busy looking at the gun and at Jim that he didn't notice Leia step quietly into the doorway. Didn't notice until she brought the kar'takin down on his wrist, cleanly separating his gun hand from his arm.

"Try holding it now!" she screamed.

Leia raised the blade again and struck at Matt's head. But her target, who accepted his injury without the slightest outward sign of pain or panic, grabbed the weapon with his remaining hand and wrenched it away. He tossed it to the floor and stood on the shaft. Then he grabbed Leia by the throat. Slowly, he lifted her off the floor.

Jim struggled to his feet. Just then the Glock discharged a round. The slug buzzed past his left ear.

The pistol lay on the floor, Matt's severed hand still wrapped around the grip. The hand twitched and rocked. It was trying to move the weapon.

Trying to aim it.

Another shot sped Jim's way, barely missing him.

"Willy!" he shouted. "Get the gun!"

The terrified red shirt dashed through the doorway. Screaming, he fell to all fours next to the weapon, grappling with the hand for control.

Another round discharged. It sped past Rayna and Gary and straight through the window, shattering it.

"Get his hand away from it!" Jim shouted.

"I'm trying!" Willy shrieked. "It won't let go!"

Leia, held a foot above the floor and slowly choking, furiously kicked her dangling, slippered feet. Jim ducked around her and punched Matt hard in the kidneys. Once, twice, a third time. Nothing happened.

He remembered his Taser. He took it out and aimed it.

That got Matt's attention. He turned, still holding Leia by the neck, and threw her at Jim. He caught her, but the impact landed them both back on the floor.

Jim managed to raise his Taser and fire. Matt jumped out of the darts' way, toward the hallway door.

Leia, still weak, regained enough of her senses to bring her own stun gun to bear. She fired but also missed.

The two of them got to their feet, weapons ready. Matt, while dodging the darts, had cornered himself in the hallway leading to the exterior door. There was only one way out.

"Thanks for coming to my party," he said as he eyed the hallway exit. "But I think it's time to call it a night. Going to be a big day tomorrow. Catch you at the convention."

Then he put his shoulder to the door, pushing it off its hinges with frightening ease. He fled into the hallway, toward the fire-exit stairs.

"Oh, shit," Jim said.

A zombie peeked inside the room and moaned. It staggered into the entry with another close behind.

"Everybody out!" Jim said. "Into the next room! Go, go, go!"

Willy ran up to him.

"I got the gun," he said, handing over the Glock.

Jim used it to put a bullet in the skull of the first zombie. He did the same to the second. But three more had found the door and were on their way in.

Rayna, Willy, and Leia helped Gary to his feet and through the connecting door. Jim expended five more rounds, dropping five more zombies. Yet still they came.

"Come on!" Leia screamed as she grabbed the kar'takin.

Jim retreated along with the others through the connecting door. Rayna and Leia were struggling to push a dresser in front of it because Jim's kick had broken the lock. There wasn't much time.

"Give me five seconds," he said.

He ran to the opposite side of the suite, to the other connecting door. He unlocked it, opened it a crack, and looked around. He found nothing but darkness. Jim pushed the door open and then felt around the wall for a light switch. The space seemed oddly warm.

"Hurry!" Rayna shouted.

The dresser was only waist high, and the undead were piling in, trying to get over the top. Leia took out her Mace and fired carefully aimed shots at the alien eyes. The first tier of undead writhed in pain, obstructing the ones behind them.

But their sheer weight began to tell. The dresser slowly slid away from the doorway.

To his immense relief, Jim realized that the next suite over was empty. The air conditioner was broken. The environmental unit under the window lay partially disassembled on the floor, where a repair worker had left it.

He ran back to the other suite, where the others were losing the battle to hold back the zombies. The doorway was a writhing mass of bloodied heads and waving arms.

"Let's move!" Jim shouted as he pulled Gary off the bed.

Gary looked around blearily. "What?"

Jim dragged him into the next room and lowered him into a sitting position on the floor. Rayna and Willy followed a moment later. Leia, carrying Jim's backpack, came last.

Jim slammed the door, locked it, then pushed another dresser in front of it.

As soon as he finished, Rayna hugged him.

"I can't believe it," she said. "I can't believe you're here."

"I told you I'd come," Jim reminded her. "Are you okay?"

"I'm not hurt, if that's what you mean," Rayna said, her eyes filling with tears. "But none of us are okay."

"I know. I know everything."

"How?"

"We found T'Poc in the stairwell. She'd been bitten, but she hadn't turned yet. She told us what happened. She said Matt could have helped her, but didn't. She warned us that he'd gone nuts."

"How could she know that?" Gary asked.

"The things inside her . . . told her. They seem to have some sort of telepathic ability. They share information."

"Great," Gary said. "Cloud-computing zombies."

"Exactly," Jim said. "T'Poc even used the word 'network.' These things are connected to some kind of central information hub."

"What did you do with T'Poc?" Rayna asked. "Where is she now?"

Jim was still fumbling for an answer when Leia stepped in. "She's in a better place now," she said. "She's lucky she ran into us when she did."

"So it's just like in the movies," Gary said forlornly. "If you're bitten by a zombie, you become one."

"Except for the eyeballs," Jim said. "Based on what T'Poc told us—and some other things we saw—I think it's a parasite. It gets into our bodies and takes over. T'Poc sort of confirmed that. She said she sensed alien thoughts inside her, controlling her."

"What did she mean by 'alien'?" Rayna asked. "You mean 'alien' as in 'strange' or 'foreign'?"

"No," Jim said. "I'm pretty sure she meant 'alien' as in 'not from Earth.'"

A long interval of shocked silence followed. Gary finally ended it.

"Da, da-da da-da, *da da*," he sang.

Rayna, Leia, and Jim looked at him reproachfully.

"What the hell was that for?" Rayna asked.

"I'm just trying to break the tension," Gary said. "If this were a *Star Trek* episode, we'd totally be going to a commercial break right now."

CHAPTER

22

THE SIEGE

From the just-abandoned next-door suite came a few not-very-determined moans. Occasionally, there was a scratching sound, or a loud thump against the door, but for the moment they appeared safe.

Jim used the opportunity to study his surroundings in detail. After facing so much blood and chaos, the room's orderly decor was disorienting. There was the bathroom on their left; a door leading to a private bedroom on their right; in front of them a kitchenette with a table; and against the far wall a seating area, complete with two chairs, a couch, and a coffee table. Rayna and Willy sat across from Leia and Jim while Gary hovered anxiously near the door. Whatever injuries he'd sustained vanished in the presence of the princess; he seemed in awe of her.

"May I bring Your Highness a bottle of water?" he asked. "I bet the minibar is full of them."

"Why don't you bring us all some water?" Jim said. "Since you're offering."

Gary practically skipped across the room and returned with five chilled bottles of Aquafina. After distributing them to the group, he remained standing at the princess's side, as if awaiting further instructions. Leia glanced at him and then pointedly turned her head. Finally, Jim stood up and whispered in Gary's ear.

"*Sack,*" he said.

Gary's face turned an alarming shade of red. He violently adjusted his uniform.

"Sorry," he said to Leia.

Leia raised her water bottle in a toast. "To Gary," she said. "For saving our lives."

"Me?" Gary replied. "What did I do?"

"When Jim and I were in that elevator, all alone, I thought he was ready to give up. But you figured out how to reach us, and suddenly we knew we weren't alone. We got our act together and found our way here."

Gary seemed to relax a little. But only a little.

"I guess I did my bit," he said. "I just wish I'd picked up on Matt sooner. He'd been acting weird ever since we got to the suite, but I didn't realize he'd gone nuts."

"Before he holed up in the bedroom, he walked around calling himself 'Commodore,'" Rayna added. "Only he actually seemed to believe it. And he was really, really upset about you guys. Especially you, Jim. He kept saying that we couldn't afford to take on passengers because it could disrupt the chain of command. He came out of the bedroom while you were heading down the hall. Didn't say a word. Just grabbed Gary by the arm, slammed him twice against the hallway wall, and tossed him aside. Then he pulled me away from the door and shut it. He held it while you tried to get in. It's like he went crazy."

"This was not crazy," Jim said. "He lost his hand and didn't make a sound. He head-butted me across the room and knocked a steel-frame door off its hinges with his shoulder. That's not crazy."

"You'd be surprised," Rayna said. "We study this stuff in my psychology classes. In cases of extreme agitation and psychosis, patients can perform feats of strength not unlike what Matt accomplished."

"He didn't seem all that agitated," Leia said. "I looked at his face while he was strangling me. There was nothing there. Murdering me was just a chore. Something to check off his to-do list."

"And his hand kept shooting the gun after it was cut off," Jim said. "How do your psychology classes explain that?"

"Look, I'm only a junior," Rayna shrugged.

"Maybe he's a runner," Gary said. "One of those super-zombies from *28 Days Later*. They move like they're in the Olympics or something. If we're up against runners, we're dead. Actually, *I'm* dead. I can't do much running. I . . . don't have the right shoes."

Leia put her feet on the coffee table, showing off her gigantic Star Trek slippers.

"You and me both," she said. "But don't worry. All the zombies we've seen are slow as Gorns."

Gary sighed with relief.

"We've got another thing going for us," Jim said. "Lights. Wherever the zombies go, they knock out the lamps. This hallway's dark. So was the third floor. The only reason the atrium's still bright is probably because they can't reach anything. The fixtures are too high."

"Why would they hate light?" Rayna asked.

"I'm not sure," Leia said. "But have you ever seen those third eyes of theirs blink?"

"I've been too busy hauling ass to notice," Gary said.

"You're right," Rayna said. "They just stare at you."

"This could come in handy," Gary said. "Maybe a bright flashlight could disorient or temporarily blind them."

"My point," Jim said, "is that these particular zombies seem to function best at night. So if we can last until dawn, we stand a much better chance of getting out of here."

"Who says we have to get out of here?" Rayna asked. "Maybe Matt was right. Maybe we just need to stay put. If the people in *Dawn of the Dead* could survive in a shopping mall, we sure as hell could do worse than staying in a hotel."

She outlined a plan with several very attractive possibilities. The first order of business would be to sneak down to the lobby and somehow find a way to reseal the front doors. Next they would pick off the zombies one by one and room by room. The corpses would be hauled to the roof and dropped off one side of the building. Then they would take their residence on the opposite side, somewhere near the Gweagal Room, for easy access to the hotel's abundant supply of food, canned soft drinks, and water. There had to be enough resources for them to survive three months, six months, maybe longer—certainly long enough for the rest of the world to sort out the apocalypse.

"That sounds like a good plan to me," Willy said. "Better 'the devil you know' and all that. At least here, we have some control."

Jim shook his head. "You guys don't know what you're talking about," he said. "To take the hotel, we'd have to eliminate hundreds, maybe thousands, of undead. I doubt I could accomplish that with a full platoon of Rangers. Certainly not without high casualties."

"They did it in *Dawn of the Dead*," Rayna shrugged.

"The *other* problem," Jim continued, "is that you're assuming the power stays on."

"I'm not assuming anything," Rayna said. "If the lights go out, we'll use candles. People survived for centuries without electricity."

"If the power goes out," Jim continued, "all of the electronically controlled doors are programmed to open. This is a basic tenet of fire safety. In the event of an emergency, you don't want to trap anyone inside the building. So we could spend all week following your plan—

but as soon as the grid goes down, it'll be open season at the Botany Bay."

Rayna went over to the window and opened the curtain. Like Donnie's room on the third floor, this one didn't feature a view of anything beyond the adjacent parking garage. "I wish we knew what was going on out there."

"I'd like to say there are millions of National Guard soldier mowing down zombies with M-16s, but that seems pretty unlikely," Gary said, sighing.

"There's one way to know for sure," Jim said. "If we can get to a corner suite, we'll have a great view of downtown Houston. We'll see everything happening outside. We'll see neighboring buildings. Maybe we can wave to someone and signal for help. And, most important, we can watch the zombies at dawn. See what the sunlight does to them. If they start to retreat when it gets light outside, I think we need to take our chance and get out while we can."

"That sounds fine," Rayna said. "But how do we get to the corner suite?"

"Using the interior connecting doors. There are three rooms separating our current position from the objective. Even if they're all full of zombies, we've got enough ammo to push our way through."

"Who's 'we'?" Gary asked.

"Leia and I," Jim said. "Or at least that's what I'd planned."

Jim turned to her.

"Are you up for this?" he asked.

"Not really," she said. "But I'll go anyway."

"I enter first, followed by Leia," Jim said. "Rayna waits at the door. If things go south, she lets us back in. Understood?"

"Understood," Rayna said.

"What about us?" Gary and Willy asked.

"You wait until the all-clear, then join us. Maybe later I'll give you some training tips. But right now, there's no time to teach you how to sweep a building for unfriendlies. So just hang back. Got it?"

"No problem," Gary said.

"Seems smart to me," Willy agreed. "Red shirts usually lead the way, and we all know how that works out."

Leia picked up her gun belt and put it on. Jim examined his Taser and checked to make sure it carried a cartridge. Then, a moment later, he checked again.

"So how are *you* doing, soldier?" Rayna asked.

"Edgy," Jim said. "Can you blame me?"

He watched Leia click her spare cartridge into her Taser.

"Maybe we'll get lucky again," Rayna said. "Maybe all three of these rooms will be empty."

"This floor is packed," Jim told her. "I looked at the check-in schedule. Odds are, we're going to meet some very unhappy guests."

As if to confirm their fears, a scratching noise wafted through the wall.

"What's that?" Gary asked.

"I'm pretty sure it isn't housekeeping," Jim said.

Next they heard a muffled moan. Then another. There were two distinct voices—one low and masculine, the other higher. Jim listened intently.

"Sounds like at least a couple of them," he said. "They're to our right. I think, based on the scratching, that they're trying to get into or out of the bedroom or bathroom."

"Are they after someone?" Leia asked. "Could there be a survivor?"

"We'll know in a minute," Jim said.

Jim quietly unlocked the door and left the keys in the knob for

Rayna.

"Good luck, you guys," Gary said. "I've played some intense first-person shooters, but this is on another level."

"It's because there's no reset button," Jim said.

He gestured for quiet, opened the door a couple of inches, and looked around.

23

mirror, mirror

The suite's lights were on, giving Jim a refreshingly unobstructed view. He spied two zombies, an adult male and an adolescent female, energetically clawing at the bathroom door.

They failed to notice him as he eased into the room. First, he looked around to make sure there were just two targets. Then he took careful aim at their backs with his Taser and fired.

The darts landed squarely between the creatures' shoulder blades. Jim applied the juice. After a few seconds of frenetic jerking, they fell to the floor and lay still.

Leia followed Jim into the room. She helped him drag the corpses away from the bathroom door and into the living area. The bodies left long trails of green slime—all that remained of their alien third eyes.

They checked the bedroom, finding it empty but in a shambles.

"Now, let's see about the bathroom," Jim said.

Leia knocked on the door. She told whoever might be inside that it was safe to come out.

No response.

Rayna watched from the doorway, holding the doorknob in a

death grip.

Leia knocked and spoke again. She turned to Jim and shrugged. He put his boot to the door and kicked it in.

"Hello?" he said as he entered.

The space looked just like every other suite bathroom in the Botany Bay: lots of white tile, a double vanity, and a large sunken tub. In this particular tub lay a woman perhaps forty years old. The only part of her body visible above the waterline was her head, cradled by an inflatable bath pillow. Her face wore an expression of serene repose. Or perhaps relief. Jim couldn't decide which.

On the near edge of the tub he noticed a small picture of what he assumed was the woman's family. She stood, smiling, beside a boy of perhaps seven, a girl of maybe fifteen, and her husband. Jim recognized the girl and the husband as the two zombies who were pounding on the door. He felt lightheaded, as if his spirit were trying desperately to flee the room on its own.

"I don't think I can look at this," Leia said.

Jim, on the other hand, couldn't look away. On the far side of the tub glittered several pieces of a small, shattered mirror. One shard was bloody. Jim figured the woman used it to slit her wrists. Trapped when her own family joined the cannibal dead, she'd done what Jim couldn't help but see as a sensible thing. She drew a hot bath, climbed in, and opened her veins.

The plan had succeeded brilliantly. The still water was livid red, charged with every drop of the woman's life force.

"Let's get out of here," Leia said.

"She's tall," he heard himself say. "Maybe her clothes would fit you."

"Jesus Christ," Leia said. "Are you kidding?"

"You need something to wear. She doesn't."

Leia walked out into the main living area. She saw Rayna, Gary, and Willy peering in from the adjacent room.

"Well?" Rayna asked.

"All clear," Leia said. "I'm going to check for clothes."

Leia opened one of the closets. Several women's garments were hanging from the rack, but the sizes appeared too small. Leia picked through them anyway, hoping to get lucky. There was something comforting about browsing a dress rack in the middle of a zombie apocalypse. She became so engrossed that she didn't immediately notice the young boy standing stock-still in the closet's farthest corner. A boy with a third eye on his right cheek. She didn't spot him until he lunged.

Leia leapt back from the door, screaming. She tripped over a nightstand and fell, landing hard on her back.

In the bathroom, Jim heard the commotion. He got up and started to run. But at the last possible moment something grabbed his ankle, sending him crashing to the floor.

He rolled over just in time to see the woman rising out of the tub, her hand still around his leg, crimson water spilling over the sides and splashing onto the floor.

He kicked the creature in the face, knocking it backward into the bath. Then he got to his feet and ran, pausing only to pull the bathroom door shut.

Taser in hand, he sprinted into the living room. He found Leia standing near Gary, who'd pushed the closet door shut before the zombie got all the way out. Its right leg and right arm flailed wildly. Gary and Willy held the door firmly against its torso, pinning it.

Leia and Rayna stood side by side. Leia leveled her Taser at the creature.

"Okay," she said. "Let it out."

Gary and Willy let go. The door slid open and the monster spilled facedown onto the floor. It was barefoot and wore what appeared to be cotton pajamas; they were covered with little versions of the original *Enterprise* series. Leia fired a dart into its shoulder and unleashed a blast of current. In seconds it was over.

"Did he touch you?" Jim asked.

She shook her head.

"How about you?" he asked Gary.

"I think I'm going to puke," he replied.

"Don't," Jim replied. "The bathroom's occupied."

In fact, they could hear the bathroom's occupant scratching furiously at the door.

"The mom?" Leia said.

"Yeah," Jim said. "I'll be right back."

Gary, Willy, and Leia listened as Jim walked back to the bathroom, pushed open the door, and fired the Taser. They heard the splash of the creature falling back into the tub.

Jim walked back into the bedroom. He looked at the body of the boy on the floor. Then he picked it up by the back of its pajama top and lugged it into the bathroom. Afterward he did the same with the bodies of the father and daughter. Then he shut the bathroom door, walked back into the kitchenette, and sat down at the table with the others.

"What did you do with them?" Leia asked.

"I just . . . lined them up," Jim said.

"Maybe we should put something over them," Gary said. "A sheet or something."

"They're dead," Jim said. "And we've already done the best thing we could possibly do by making sure they stay that way. Don't think about it. Just push it into the back of your mind. I know it sounds impossible, but trust me, it's the only way to handle stuff like this."

"Will it stay in the back of my mind?" Leia asked.

"No," Rayna said. "It won't."

"It will stay there long enough. Right now we've got bigger issues to deal with."

"Like what?" Gary asked.

"Like the fact that Leia nearly bought it because I was careless," Jim said. "I *saw* the boy in the photograph. I knew this room belonged to a family of four, and that only three of the family members were accounted for. But did I do the math? Did I stop to think for a minute? No."

"You can't blame yourself," Leia told him. "I should have checked the closet when I opened it."

"I *do* blame myself," Jim said. "It was my idea to go to the corner suite. My plan."

"We'll just be more careful going forward," Willy assured him. "Maybe we call out to the zombies before we open the door. Round them up, if you know what I mean. Get their attention so nobody sneaks up on us."

"Now there's an idea," Gary said. He went up to the connecting door and tapped on it. "Hello?" he called. "Anybody in there? Hello, hello?"

In response came a loud, forceful knocking from the other side. Gary recoiled so quickly that he lost his balance and fell backward. Willly let out a short scream.

"Don't shoot!" a voice shouted back. "I'm innocent!"

Gary pushed himself to his feet. "A talking zombie?"

"There's no such thing," Leia said. "That's a talking human."

24

WOLF IN THE FOLD

"Are you okay?" Jim shouted through the door.

"It was self-defense," the voice called back. "I didn't do it on purpose!"

Jim and Leia exchanged quizzical glances.

"I'm not police," Jim stated loudly. "I work with the hotel. I don't care what you did or who you did it to. But I need to get into your room, okay?"

"All right."

"Take three steps backward. I have a passkey, and I'm going to open the door."

"All right," the voice repeated, slightly fainter this time.

Jim took the key from Rayna, unlocked the door, and opened it.

He was confronted by a massive Klingon in full battle armor. A massive Klingon that, judging from his bloodshot eyes and the moistness of his cheeks, had been crying.

"Martock," Jim said.

The Klingon looked at his rescuers, then burst into tears again.

"It was self-defense," he said between sobs. "She would have killed me. She was like some kind of monster."

He wrapped his gigantic arms around Jim, buried his head on his right shoulder, and continued weeping.

Jim patted him on the back, let him cry for a few moments, and then spoke.

"You mean the girl in your booth," he said. "The one who was sleeping on your cot."

"Her name was Karen," Martock said. "I kept telling her to go up to our room. She was so sick. But she wouldn't move. After the vendor area shut down, I started packing up the booth, putting away my valuables, and somehow I lost track of her. Couldn't find her anywhere. The place was deserted and her cot was empty. I was rushing because I had to bring a commission to the Klingon Feast—"

"Matt's bat'leth," Gary remarked.

Jim motioned for him to keep quiet. "And then what?"

"I was getting ready to leave when I heard something behind my booth. Something rummaging behind the partition. I pulled it aside and saw Karen on her hands and knees on the floor. At first my mind refused to accept what it saw. But then I realized that she was crouching *over* someone. A body. A body whose stomach had been cut open. Both of her hands were filled with intestines, and as I watched she brought the pile up to her bloody mouth and took a bite. And then . . . then she came after me."

"Let's go sit down," Jim suggested.

He guided Martock back to the dining area table. The five of them sat down.

"I didn't know what was wrong," Martock continued. "I didn't know what to do. I mean, what's the procedure when your good friend suddenly turns into a cannibal?"

"I'm guessing you run," Leia offered.

"That's right," Martock said. "I backed away, almost tripping over the damn cot. She followed me. She was moaning. It was horrible. I ran away with the bat'leth still in my hands. I ran to the men's room and hid in one of the stalls. Just waited in there, with my feet up on the toilet. Maybe a minute or two later I heard the door open. And like an idiot I said, 'Who's there?' All I heard in reply was moaning. I heard her slowly stagger through the bathroom. I saw her feet go by. They were bloody. Once she got past I decided to open the door and run for it. But just as I did, I caught sight of her. And she of me. And then I noticed something that was a thousand times worse than the blood or the moaning."

"The eye," Jim said. "The red one."

"That's right," Martock said. "She had a huge third eye on her forehead. Somehow I knew that it was responsible for what happened. For what she'd become. I got mad. I swung the bat'leth and I . . . ."

"I know," Jim said. "You took her head. I saw the body."

"I dropped the bat'leth in the men's room and ran," Martock said. "I know this sounds crazy, but if you look behind my booth you'll see what she did. She was like an animal."

"You mean you've been up here this whole time *hiding from the police*?" Jim asked. "You have no idea what's going on? You haven't heard any of the noise from the hallway?"

Martock removed a bloodied MP3 player from his pocket. "For the last few hours I've been alone with Jerry Goldsmith and James Horner, savoring my last few hours of freedom," he said.

"Well, there's good news and bad news," Gary said cheerfully. "Which do you want to hear first?"

They broke it down for him quickly. The good news was that he wasn't going to jail. The bad news was that the world was ending. All things considered, the Klingon seemed relieved.

"What happens now?" he asked.

"We're working on it," Jim said. "Is there anyone else in your suite?"

"No, it was just me and Karen. We'd bunk together at conventions to save money."

"Wait, Karen Masterson?" Leia asked. "The costume designer?"

Martock nodded. "I thought your bikini looked familiar. That's one of Karen's pieces, isn't it?"

"I hired her to make it for me," Leia said. "But if it's okay with you, I'd like to exchange it for something else. It's not really practical under the circumstances."

"Help yourself," Martock said. "I'm sure Karen wouldn't mind."

Leia patted him on the shoulders and entered the adjoining room. Meanwhile, Jim introduced Martock to the rest of his crew and briefed him on the plan to invade the corner suite.

"I've been thinking about something you told me downstairs," Jim said. "When I was looking at your weapons in the vending area, you said you had a few live blades up in your bedroom."

"More than a few," Martock began.

Before he could elaborate, Leia emerged from the adjoining suite. Gary gasped and grabbed Jim's forearm. She'd changed into what he recognized as Princess Leia's outfit from the opening moments of the original *Star Wars*—a hooded, all-white robe cinched around her waist with a silver belt.

"What do you think?" she said. "It even came with shoes."

"It's spectacular," Gary sputtered.

"I'm just glad I found something in my size," Leia shrugged. She glanced at the tag that was dangling from her sleeve and then said, "Mr. Michael Bigalow of Dallas is going to be very disappointed when he learns I've taken his commission."

Rayna laughed. "Michael Bigalow's a drag queen," she said. "He puts on these really funny burlesque shows. There's a female Time Lord called Dr. Who-ha, and then a nymphomaniac Borg called Sixty of Nine."

"Well, I'm guessing tonight's performance is canceled," Leia said. She tore the tag off the sleeve and tossed it aside.

"Wear it with honor," Martock said.

"I will," Leia said. "And just wait until you see the accessories." She ducked into the adjoining suite and returned a moment later with a four-foot-long staff; one end formed a club and the other featured a fan-shaped blade.

Jim glanced at Martock. "Please tell me that's real."

"It's a *lirpa*," Martock said. "A Vulcan ceremonial weapon first seen in the original *Trek* episode, 'Amok Time.'"

"You don't have to sell me on it," Jim said. "Got any more?"

"You can help yourself," Martock said. "Everything's in our suite. Just be careful because it's all live."

Jim, Leia, Willy, and Gary walked next door.

"Merry Christmas, guys," Leia said.

"And a Happy New Year," Jim replied as he surveyed the suite's contents.

The center of the public area was mostly taken up by two long, wheeled racks filled with garment bags. But Jim was more interested in the hardware arrayed on the kitchenette table.

He saw four wicked-looking swords that he recognized as *yan*— Klingon ceremonial blades. He picked one up, checked its edge, and then took a couple experimental swings. Gary and Willy grabbed two more and started to play-fight.

"Nobody touch my lirpa," Leia said.

"I wouldn't think of touching it," Jim said. "At least not until the third date."

Gary laughed but Leia seemed disconcerted.

"So that's how this works?" she asked.

"How what works?" Jim said as he continued testing the sword.

"We break into a room and put down an entire family of zombies that were living human beings not too long ago. And then a few minutes later we're goofing around with play swords and I'm telling you not to touch my lirpa. Is that how this works?"

"That's pretty much it," Jim said. "You push down the stuff that's already happened to make room for the stuff that comes next."

"I see," Leia said. "How hard can you push before it pushes back?"

"You can ask that question to a therapist," Jim said. "Assuming the world goes back to normal and we still have therapists."

"I want a bat'leth," Gary said. "Can I have a bat'leth?"

"No," Jim replied. "Nobody gets a weapon until they have a chance to practice with it. That means you, mister."

Gary frowned and put down his sword.

"The princess gets a weapon," he said. "She didn't have to practice."

"She gets extra credit for real-world experience," Jim replied. "As for the rest of you, nobody gets so much as a pair of toenail clippers until we go over some basics. If it's any consolation, we're sticking with Tasers when we hit the corner suite."

"Are we still doing that?" Leia asked.

"We're just one door away. We'd be crazy not to take the chance."

Gary walked to the interior door that opened to the corner suite and put his ear against it.

"I don't hear anything," he said.

"Maybe that's good," Jim said. "But maybe not. These things seem pretty lethargic when there's nothing to eat. A dozen of them could be milling around over there, waiting for room service to arrive."

Gary shook his head. "You're the king of the worst-case scenarios."

"When you plan for the worst, sometimes you're pleasantly surprised," Jim said. "Now let's put on our game faces and get this done."

Jim unholstered his Taser and nodded to Leia, who took up position behind him. Then he unlocked the door as quietly as possible, pushed it open an inch, looked around, and stepped inside.

The lights were on. Nothing was out of place. Against the far wall, Jim could see a bank of curtained windows.

He looked to his left. Sitting on an overstuffed chair was a man with a laptop computer balanced on his knees. He snapped it shut and stared at Jim, mouth agape.

Jim stared back.

"Say something," the man finally said.

Jim smiled. "Dr. Sandoval, I presume?"

The man exhaled, seemingly relieved. "At your service."

CHAPTER

25

BY INFERNO'S LIGHT

A few minutes later, Jim and the rest of his group stood together on the balcony of the corner suite, taking their first look at downtown Houston.

"We're in deep shit," Gary said. "Deep like the Mariana Trench."

"We can't leave here," Rayna said. "There's no place to go."

Their perch provided a peek inside the glass-clad skyscrapers surrounding the Botany Bay. Some were dark, but others still had lights, making it easy to see the zombies inside, wandering listlessly through drab, cubicle-filled spaces. In one meeting room a pack of the undead gnawed on a corpse splayed across an oval conference table. Down the street, a Doubletree Hotel was burning furiously, its top floors swathed in smoke and flame. No one fought the blaze.

"This really is the Apocalypse," Leia said.

"It could be worse," Jim said. He pointed due east, past the dark, still body of water known as the Houston Ship Channel. The horizon was lit up bright as dawn by a raging inferno. "That's Baytown Complex—one of the world's largest petrochemical refineries. They process half a million barrels of oil every day."

The smell of burning gasoline hung heavy in the air.

"I don't think they'll make their quota today," Gary said.

"That fire is on the other side of the San Jacinto River," Jim said. "Whatever this plague might be, it's spreading. Maybe it's everywhere."

"This is unbelievable," Rayna said. "Look over there."

She pointed to a sleek-looking, gray streetcar, part of the city's METRORail system, laying on its side with every topside window broken out. The car looked to be at least a hundred feet long and had to weigh several tons. Yet somehow the creatures had knocked it off the tracks and tipped it over.

"There's strength in numbers," Jim said. "On an individual level, no single zombie is very strong. But they seem to understand that they can work as a team. Like army ants. They can network their thoughts and plan a coordinated attack."

Which doesn't bode well for us, he was about to continue, but then his gaze landed on a young man staring through a window in a nearby office building. The guy wore a pair of khaki pants and a blue, short-sleeved polo shirt. Earlier that very day, he had probably been someone's office intern.

Now, missing a left hand and a considerable portion of face, he was a zombie. A zombie with a third eye sprouting out of its right cheek.

A third eye that, Jim realized, was looking at him.

The creature pounded on one of the office's floor-to-ceiling windows. He was shortly joined by three more undead, all of whom commenced moaning and pounding.

Jim pointed them out.

"Watch this," he said.

A moment later the much-abused window finally gave way. It fell to the street and shattered. The glass was quickly followed by the zombie intern in the blue polo shirt. Utterly infatuated by the sight of the

Botany Bay survivors, it mindlessly stepped out into nothingness.

The other zombies likewise tumbled into the void. Then another undead creature shambled to the window, spotted Jim, started moaning, and fell.

"We'd better go inside," he said. "We're attracting too much attention."

"Seriously?" Gary said. "I could watch those dipshits walk the plank all night."

Jim pointed to another building. Zombies on three floors were staring at them. Here and there, in one location and another, the creatures were becoming aware of their existence. He wondered how long it would be until every flesh-eater, everywhere, was giving them the big red eye.

"Why are they looking at us?" Willy asked.

"Isn't it obvious?" Jim said. "We're all that's left. And right now they're uploading their discovery to the network."

"I've seen enough," Gary decided. "Let's go in."

They stepped back into the cool, quiet refuge of the Botany Bay's seventh-floor corner suite.

"How's the view?" Dr. Sandoval asked.

The events of the last six hours had left him physically unscathed. His Starfleet uniform was still immaculate. He was still the spitting image of the *Voyager*'s doctor.

"I've seen better," Jim said. "How long has it been like this?"

"During the day I could tell that something was happening. But it wasn't until evening that I understood the scope—and the nature—of the crisis. After sunset the reanimates were free to move outdoors. They pursued and consumed every living thing they encountered."

"We notice that they seem to like the darkness," Leia said.

"I wouldn't say they 'like' it, but it's certainly a better environment for them," Sandoval said. "Their crude, parasitic eyes lack retinas with which to regulate light intake."

Jim and the rest stared at him.

"How do you know that?" Gary asked.

"I'm an exobiologist. I work for the Special Projects Office of the Defense Advance Research Projects Agency, which is part of the Department of Defense."

"Right, but you sound like you've dissected one of these things," Rayna said.

"I've been studying these creatures for the better part of a decade. I was scheduled to present a paper about their ocular adaptations at the convention."

"You were going to tell the world about these things at Gulf-Con?" Jim said.

"No. I was going to give the Trekkies a boilerplate speech about whether the life forms in the Trek universe could actually exist. My research findings were for the *real* convention."

"The real convention?" Rayna said.

"Correct," Sandoval said. "The much smaller, highly classified gathering for which GulfCon serves as a front."

Sandoval surveyed the stunned faces surrounding him, then sighed.

"I suppose I'd better start at the beginning," he said.

CHAPTER

26

NOTHING HUMAN

"The rest of you might want to sit down," Sandoval said. "I'll bring you up to speed as fast as I can, but it will take a couple of minutes."

They dutifully gathered in the seating area next to the windows. Martock sat apart from the group, still sulking. Sandoval remained standing.

"Let me tell you a little bit about GulfCon," he said. "This convention is the one and only event staged by a Dallas-based marketing outfit called Star Unlimited. Star is a front corporation for a Newark, New Jersey–based firm called Horizons Exports, which ships sensitive products and materials to overseas governments and organizations. Horizon, in turn, is a subsidiary of STNG Corp., a multinational conglomerate with its fingers in everything from private security to military-base construction."

"I met some of those guys in Afghanistan," Jim said. "We called them Stingers. They were real assholes."

"Perhaps, but they know how to keep secrets. That's why they get so much business from a Langley, Virginia, organization called the Central Intelligence Agency."

"Wait a minute," Rayna said. "You're telling me that the CIA sponsors GulfCon?"

"Precisely."

"Damn," Gary said. "I didn't realize Trekkies were a national security threat."

"They're not," Sandoval continued. "But they do provide ideal camouflage. For the past five years we've used GulfCon as a cover for a smaller convention-within-a-convention—a select gathering of scientists, military men, and covert operatives from across the United States."

"That's ridiculous," Gary said. "Couldn't you just e-mail each other?"

"The matters we discuss are too sensitive. Every August roughly fifty of us convene here in person. We dress up like Trekkies and try to get into the spirit of the event, which helps our cover. Whoever comes as the most obscure character actually wins a prize."

"What's so obscure about you?" Willy said. "You're the emergency medical hologram from *Voyager*. Everybody knows that."

"Ah, except I'm not," Sandoval said. "I'm the emergency medical hologram on the *Enterprise-E* from the movie *First Contact*. My uniform is slightly different. Study stills from the film and you'll see."

"That's pretty dastardly," Gary said. "I salute you."

"What do you talk about at this convention-in–a-convention?" Jim asked.

Sandoval pointed to the window.

"Them," he said. "Or, more accurately, the things that made them."

"You know what they are?" Jim said. "Tell us. Tell us everything."

"All right," Sandoval said. "The information I'm about to share is classified, but given current circumstances, I think full disclosure is in order. Please hold your questions until the end. We're facing a dead-line, so I need to disseminate this quickly."

"Deadline?" Jim said. "What kind of . . . ?"

Sandoval held up his right hand for silence, then began.

"Are any of you familiar with Project Genesis?" he asked.

"*Wrath of Khan*!" Willy exclaimed, like he was answering the final question of a Star Trek trivia bowl. "It's the process that trans-formed lifeless planets into life-bearing ones."

Sandoval shook his head.

"No, I'm speaking of the *real* Project Genesis, a 2001 NASA mis-sion that collected solar wind samples and then returned them to earth in a small reentry capsule."

"I can't wait to hear what this has to do with zombies," Leia said.

"During reentry, the Genesis capsule's parachute failed to open. It impacted the ground at Dugway Proving Ground in Utah doing just shy of two hundred miles per hour. The malfunction was publicly blamed on a design flaw. In reality, the ship hit a meteor shower; we were lucky to get it back at all. Three of the rocks were trapped in the ship's collectors and returned to Earth. They were complex, silica-based nodules of almost uniform size. We scooped them up, took them to the Johnson Spaceflight Center, and put them in a clean room. We didn't know what we had. We were trying to protect *them* from *us*."

"So what did you have?" Jim asked.

"To put it simply, space seeds. God knows how long they'd drifted through the void, seeking a place to take root."

"But they were rocks," Gary said. "How could they be alive?"

"We discovered their true nature when we cut one in half," San-doval said. "A technician was somehow exposed during the process, ei-ther inhaling or perhaps ingesting a bit of the material. Within three hours he was sick. Within another two he was dead. And shortly after that . . . "

"The first zombie," Gary said.

"The first *reanimate*," Sandoval corrected. "Fortunately, this happened on-site. We contained him as soon as we realized—and forced ourselves to accept—the truth. Still, the situation almost got out of control. The technician, whom we later designated Patient One, bit two medical workers and a security guard before being subdued. All of them fell sick, died, and reanimated. This, to put it mildly, changed the tenor of our investigation."

"You should have shot them back into space," Jim said.

"The material was deemed too dangerous even to move. The government constructed a secret underground containment facility at Johnson. That's where I've spent the past five years."

"What did you learn?" Rayna asked.

"We exposed the samples to various plants and animals to ascertain the threat they posed to terrestrial life. We determined that each alien cell—and I use the term 'cell' loosely, because their internal workings have nothing in common with ours—can produce reanimation within twelve hours of ingestion. The victims died and then resurrected, always with an extra eye. The process didn't work on reptiles, amphibians, fish, and other lower life forms. Their neural networks are too primitive to handle the rewiring the aliens do."

"What sort of rewiring?" Rayna asked.

"They shut down things like breathing and high-order mental acuity. But they keep motor ability. Or rather, the best motor ability a walking corpse can manage. The aliens can only get their hosts to move at a slow walk."

"So, no runners then," Gary said.

"Excuse me?" Sandoval replied.

"You know, fast zombies that can really haul ass," Gary said.

Sandoval smiled a weary smile.

"No runners," he said.

"Did you try to communicate with them?" Jim asked.

"Of course. We quickly realized they aren't sentient. All they want, really, is to ... "

"Eat?" Rayna said.

"Actually no," Sandoval continued. "Their nutritional needs are met by a type of photosynthesis. Give them a bit of pretty much anything from the back end of the electromagnetic spectrum, from ultraviolet to microwaves, and they're good."

"So what's with the biting?" Jim asked.

"It's a form of reproduction. They need hosts to reproduce, and their mode of infection is ingenious. They destroy most of an infectee's brain, but keep the portion responsible for motor functions and hunger. The reanimates are inflamed by a primal urge to consume other creatures."

"How does this help with reproduction?" Gary asked.

"They're driven by an overwhelming desire to hunt, but they aren't very good at it. They're slow and physically weak. So most often, unless they surprise or corner their prey, all they can manage is a bite or two before their 'meal' gets away. Those would-be victims then crawl into a corner, die, and rise again—under new management, of course."

"Reproduction via a crappy hunting strategy," Gary said. "That's not a very elegant approach."

Sandoval gestured toward the window.

"But it works," he said.

"I don't suppose you developed a vaccine," Jim said.

"I'm afraid not. The disease is universally fatal. We learned this by studying forty-six intentionally infected animal specimens, plus seven accidentally infected humans."

"Seven?" Rayna said. "You only mentioned four."

"After the incident with Patient One, we instituted extreme safeguards. But in spite of those, the organisms managed to reach three more people. When it became apparent that they were still taking victims even under highly controlled conditions, active study ceased. Now we focus on containment. Or at least we did, until this week."

"How did they get out?" Gary asked.

"I don't know all the details, because I wasn't there when it happened. On Wednesday evening at 5:12 p.m. a massive computer anomaly opened the doors to the containment facilities. Many of the specimens they housed hadn't been examined in years. It wasn't worth the risk."

"What caused the computer failure?" Gary asked.

"It might have been a cyberattack. Though I wonder if the aliens themselves were responsible. After seeing the insidious approaches they've used to infect biological entities, I can't dismiss the idea that they found some way to infiltrate the complex's computers."

"So if all hell is breaking loose, why did you come to GulfCon?" Jim asked.

"Given what happened, the gathering was even more important. Plus, at first there seemed no need for urgency. In case of general contamination, the facility was equipped with a fail-safe mechanism. A thermobaric bomb that incinerated everything in the bunker."

"That's the accident they've been talking about on the news," Jim said.

"Correct. The bomb was powerful enough to vaporize all organic and semiorganic matter. But not quite powerful enough, in theory, to penetrate the facility's six-foot-thick outer wall. In the event of containment loss, it could turn the place into a crematory."

"And yet . . . here we are, hiding from zombies," Rayna said.

"Indeed," Sandoval said. "Approximately two dozen people from the Johnson Spaceflight Center were slated to attend this convention. One of them, or perhaps more, was infected and carried the alien plague to Houston. I suspect it was Colonel Oliver Cronin, the base security chief, but that hasn't been confirmed."

"What was his costume?" Gary asked.

Sandoval seemed amused by the digression. "He came as Bele, from the original series episode, 'Let That Be Your Last Battlefield.' He was a big fan of the old *Batman* TV series."

"Bele, the *Star Trek* character, was a big *Batman* fan?" Jim asked impatiently.

"No, Colonel Oliver Cronin, the base security chief, was a big fan of the old *Batman* series. The actor who played the Riddler on that show was . . . "

"Oh! I know! Frank Gorshin!" Gary exclaimed.

"Exactly. Frank Gorshin played the Riddler, but he also played Bele. It was a fairly easy costume for our colonel to put together. All he had to do was paint half his face black and the other half white and acquire a silver jumpsuit."

"I remember this episode," Rayna said. "It was about two guys fighting an interplanetary race war. One group in their society had black on the right side of their faces and white on the other, and the other group had the exact opposite arrangement."

"Really a dumb paint-by-numbers premise," Gary mused. "It bordered on self-parody."

"And yet Gorshin received an Emmy nomination for his role," Willy pointed out.

"Which was stupid," Gary shot back. "They give the guy who was black on the right side an Emmy nod, while the guy who was black on the *left* side, who did exactly the same amount of work . . . "

"Lou Antonio," Willy said.

"Yeah, black-on-the-left-side Lou didn't get squat," Gary continued, indignant.

Sandoval tried to follow the banter, his head cocked to the side like a dog that's heard a strange sound.

"I'm afraid we've tumbled down the rabbit hole," he said.

Jim took a deep breath and let it out slowly. He contemplated telling Gary and Willy to shut up, but then decided not to. Better they focus on Lou Antonio's résumé instead of deliberating too much about the horrors surrounding them.

"I'm pretty sure Colonel Cronin made it to GulfCon," Jim said. "Earlier this afternoon, my security chief received complaints about a drunk mime. The guy was staggering around and banging on doors. The police took him away, which means he probably infected an entire precinct single-handedly."

"An otherwise-healthy specimen feels symptoms three to four hours after infection," Sandoval said. "Physical decline progresses rapidly after that. Death occurs within twelve hours, and reanimation shortly thereafter. If the infected subject is killed in the initial attack, reanimation can take place almost immediately."

"Why?" Rayna asked.

"It's easier to steal the house if no one's home to defend it," Sandoval said. "The parasites also work more quickly in the presence of an EM source. The 'food' matures them faster."

Jim sighed. None of this was helping.

"There's a lot you guys don't know," Rayna said. "Haven't you had years to study these things?'

"I'll answer your question with a question," Sandoval said. "What initially attracted you to Star Trek?"

"I thought Patrick Stewart was hot," Rayna said.

"Fair enough. You know what I always liked? The inevitable moment when some horrible crisis threatened to destroy the ship, and there seemed no way out. And then, suddenly, at the last possible second, Scotty or Geordi LaForge or B'Elanna Torres or Chief O'Brien would get a faraway look in their eyes and spout some long, long line of techno-babble about venting the plasma from the warp nacelles or—"

"—recalibrating the dilithium crystals," Willy offered.

"—ejecting the warp core," added Gary, once more fully engaged.

"Exactly," Sandoval continued. "And they would make these changes instantly, by pressing a few buttons, and it always worked. I loved that. I loved the idea that no matter how grave the situation, a technological solution could always bail you out. Even McCoy got in on the act. They'd need a poison antidote or a vaccine for a new disease, and he'd have it before the credits rolled, with time left over to banter with Spock. But now that I'm actually a scientist, do you know what I've learned about the Star Trek approach?"

"What?" Jim asked.

"It only works on *Star Trek*. In *this* space-time continuum, you can focus a lot of computers and a lot of great minds on a problem, and still not find a quick answer. It can take a year. Or ten years. You have to keep hammering away until the nut cracks."

"I don't think we have that much time," Leia said.

"Precisely. Given the stakes, a more rough-and-ready approach is in order. Which is why we have to get out of here."

"What do you mean?" Jim asked.

"Right now a group of very powerful people is fighting to stop this plague from spreading. And they aren't approaching the problem like Federation scientists. They're more like Klingons. They'll employ a strategy of containment and annihilation. Houston is lost. They'll cordon off the area and liquidate everyone, survivors and infected alike."

"That's pretty hardcore," Gary said.

"The danger is too great to do otherwise. If this contagion spreads, it could overwhelm the world. The government will seal off the city and then perhaps provide a short grace period to allow uninfected humans to escape. And then . . . "

"Ah, shit," Jim said. "They're going to nuke us."

"I'm guessing they'll use a fusion bomb. Turn the entire area into a sheet of glass. It's the only way to be sure."

The room grew quiet. All talk about Lou Antonio abruptly ceased.

"I thought the aliens fed on radiation," Rayna said.

"Only the low-frequency types," Sandoval said. "The highly energetic stuff put out by atomic weapons—gamma rays and the like—is as lethal to them as it is to us. Especially in their current, more or less organic forms. The EM pulse accompanying the explosion might also be disastrous. Electrical current can disrupt the neural link with their hosts."

"That explains why our Tasers work," Jim said.

"So what should we do?" Rayna asked.

"Evacuate," Sandoval said. "It's our only hope."

"Destroy Houston to save the world," Gary said. "I guess the needs of the many really do outweigh the needs of the few."

"Except we're not talking about a few," Jim said. "There are five or six million people in the Houston area. This is the fourth-largest city in the United States."

"Not for long," Sandoval said.

"When will they launch?" Jim asked.

"I'm guessing sunrise," Sandoval said. "They'll want daylight for damage assessment."

"Can't you contact them and request extraction?" Jim asked.

"I did, via a scrambled satellite uplink. It's pretty much the only method, given the loss of Internet and cell phone coverage. They responded by downloading a worm into my computer that fried my hard drive. That's the government's way of telling you that you're expendable."

"No, you're not," Jim said. "None of us are expendable. Especially a scientist who understands these creatures. We need to get out of here. We need some vehicles."

"Don't look at me," Leia said. "I took a cab."

Jim went to the windows and peered down to the street. He had a pickup truck down in the Botany Bay's garage, but there weren't enough seats to hold everyone.

"What we need is Matt's RV. It's in the garage. Easy to access, and there's room for all of us."

"You're forgetting that Matt has the keys," Gary said. "Maybe we can track him down and ask if he'll give us a ride. Hell, I'll even pump the gas again."

Rayna smiled at Gary. "And *you're* forgetting that I'm the helmsman of the USS *Stockard*." She produced a key ring from her pocket and tossed it to Jim. "And in that official capacity I am charged with carrying a second set of keys."

"Great," Jim said. "We have our ride. Now all we have to do is get to the garage without the zombies ripping us to pieces."

"Stay positive," Rayna said. "Things could always be worse."

Just then the lights went out.

"You were saying?" Jim said.

CHAPTER

27

THE MEASURE OF A MAN

The group stood silently in darkness, breathlessly willing the lights to flicker back to life. Finally, Sandoval spoke the ugly but obvious truth.

"We're at an even bigger disadvantage now," he said. "The reanimates see extremely well in low-light conditions. We don't."

"What are we going to do?" Willy said. "The hallways will be pitch black. We won't see the zombies until they're on top of us."

"The hotel's emergency lights kick on if the power fails," Jim said. "Plus we have a couple of flashlights and our Tasers have LEDs."

"If we switch those on, we might as well yell, 'Here we are, come and eat us,'" Gary said. "It will draw them like moths. Big, stinky, flesh-eating moths."

"I wish we could wait until dawn," Leia said. "It might drive those things back into the cracks and crevices."

Jim looked at Sandoval. He shook his head.

"This area will likely be ashes by then," he said.

"Then we have to play the hand we've been dealt," Jim said.

He looked at his watch.

"It's four thirty," he said. "Let's be ready to move by five. Any questions?"

"Well . . . yeah," Willy said. "How do we get to the basement?"

"What should we take?" Rayna asked.

"Who gets Tasers and who gets swords?" Gary asked.

Jim surveyed their worried faces. He'd been in this kind of situation before. He knew when people needed advice and leadership and a morale boost. But they were looking at the wrong guy.

"Hey, I'm just the bellhop," he said. "I know the hotel, and I can lead the way to the garage. But I'm not making any promises. Stop looking at me like I'm some kind of Dahar master."

Then he walked out of the suite and through the connecting door to Martock's room.

"What was that?" Gary said to Rayna. "I thought your brother was G.I. Joe."

"I'll talk to him," Rayna said.

She followed Jim into Martock's suite. She found him staring out the windows, silhouetted by the weak illumination filtering in from the atrium.

"What are you doing?" she said.

Jim was staring down at the atrium's floor. He could just make out the chair he'd fallen asleep in a lifetime ago. His newspaper sat neatly beside it. He mused that maybe this was all just a bad dream. Maybe this was one of those awful horror movies where the hero is shaken awake in the final frames, only to learn that the preceding ninety minutes have just been a long, terrible nightmare.

"Nothing," he finally answered. "Just checking the emergency lights. They're not very bright, but we should have enough to see by."

"Well, if you were trying to demotivate everyone back there, you did a pretty good job. You made sitting around and waiting to die sound appealing."

"Maybe it is."

"What are you talking about?" Rayna said.

"We won't reach the basement without casualties," he said. "Some of us, maybe all of us, will die."

"Why are you being such a pessimist?" Rayna asked. "We go downstairs, we get in the RV, and we leave. Mission accomplished."

"You left something out. The part where we have to outrun and outfight however many of those flesh-eating assholes get in our way. If there's too many of them, then that RV might as well be parked on Ceti Alpha V."

"So what should we do?"

"Maybe nothing. Maybe we should get the booze out of the minibars and have a party. Get bombed before we get bombed. At least it would be painless."

"That's insane," Rayna said.

"Then you'll really hate my other idea. We get everybody *else* drunk, then you, me and Leia make a run for the garage. Our chances are better without the others."

"That's not true," Rayna said. "Remember how Gary figured out how to contact you when you were trapped? Or how Willy drew off the zombies by sending down the elevator? Without them you probably wouldn't be here."

"I'm grateful," Jim said. "But they're not strong enough for what's ahead. They'll slow us down. Maybe get us killed."

"There's all kinds of strength, Jim," Rayna said.

"Yeah, yeah, yeah. Infinite diversity in infinite combinations."

"You remember that?"

"Of course. I also remember something I learned in the army—embrace the suck. It means, don't whine about the hand you've been dealt. Just deal with it. Right now."

"There's a part of you that's loving this," Rayna said, her voice rising. "You're finally back in your element."

Jim shot his sister a lethal look.

"There's no part of me that's loving this," he said. "Because it looks to me as if the only choice I've got is between seeing my sister fried in a nuclear blast or torn apart by zombies."

"There's got to be another way," Rayna said. "There always is."

"There might be if this were a *Star Trek* episode, but it's not. This is a zombie movie. The rules are different."

"Enlighten me," Rayna said.

"*Star Trek* is all about applying the Federation's high-minded ideals to difficult situations," Jim said. "No matter how bad things get, you're supposed to play by the don't-shoot-first, don't-mess-with-pre-warp cultures, don't-alter-the-timeline rules. But in the zombie universe, it's all about jettisoning everything—morality, sentimentality, weaklings—that might keep you from seeing the next sunrise. Because no matter how impeccably you behave, you'll never bring the other side around to your way of thinking. They don't think. They just kill."

"You can't push aside everything that makes you human just because there's a crisis," Rayna said. "If the only way to beat the zombies is to emulate them, we don't deserve to win."

"Who says we can win? Did you see what's happening outside? What if the rest of the world is just like this?"

"What if it isn't? The point is, *we don't know*. The rest of the planet could be just fine. The only way to find out is to see for ourselves. And that won't happen until you get off your morbid, self-pitying ass and take charge."

"Then it isn't going to happen."

"Well, I'm leaving. Your only choice is whether or not you want to help me."

Jim studied his sister's face.

"You'd do it, wouldn't you?" he said.

"Try me."

Jim looked at Rayna a moment longer. Long enough to decide he believed her.

"All right then," he said. "We'll go together. I guess none of my gloom and doom made an impression."

"Nope," Rayna said. "I'm a Trekkie. We don't do despair."

Jim took his sister in his arms and hugged her.

"Be careful," she said. "Don't smear my makeup."

"You're kidding, right? At this point who gives a crap?"

"I do," Rayna said. "It took a long time to apply. And until Monday morning, when GulfCon is officially over, I'm an Andorian."

"GulfCon looks pretty damn 'over' to me."

"No it isn't," Rayna replied, eyeing her brother steadily. "Not for me."

Jim stood in the dark for a moment, watching as his sister retreated to the corner suite. He suddenly understood that her blue makeup was more than a thin layer of pigment. It was a force field holding the horrors around her at bay. A warp bubble of denial that kept her functioning while so many others—himself included—stumbled.

If she could do it, perhaps the others could, too. Maybe an appeal to their Trekkie-ness was just what they needed to meld them into something approaching a fighting force. Or at least a cohesive unit with a chance of escaping the Botany Bay Hotel and Slaughterhouse alive.

He needed a way to focus their minds.

Jim walked over to the racks of new costumes and started opening garment bags. He took out his phaser, pulled its trigger, and examined the clothing by its warm red light. After opening the sixth one and seeing nothing of use, he started to feel foolish. Then, in the seventh, he found what he wanted.

Exactly what he wanted.

He took off his hotel uniform, tossed it on the floor, and started changing. He was almost done when Leia entered the room.

"What are you doing?" she asked.

"Getting into character. What are *you* doing?"

"Looking for you. This might be the last time I have you alone for a while."

Leia walked up to Jim. He'd managed to put on everything except his shirt.

"There's something I've been wondering," she said. "How do you feel about cross-genre relationships?"

It took Jim a moment to realize what she was asking. Then he smiled. "I'm going to be honest with you," he said. "I hear it's pretty difficult to make them work. You'll want to name the dog Wicket, but I'm going to call him Worf. How would you expect to find middle ground?"

"Maybe like this," she said, leaning forward and kissing him. Jim pulled her close. This time he was ready to savor it, and again, for a brief instant, it didn't feel like they were in a zombie movie anymore. They weren't in a video game and they weren't in a *Star Trek* episode. They were someplace far better, far more real—but it lasted only a moment, and then Leia broke the embrace.

"Maybe it could work," he agreed. "But we won't know for sure unless we get out of here. And to do that, we've got to get the people in the next room motivated."

"How?"

"By giving them what they need: a captain."

"Finally!" Leia exclaimed.

"That's why I decided to ditch my hotel uniform."

"That wasn't a uniform," Leia said. "*That* was a costume. It was you pretending to be something you weren't."

Jim pulled on his shirt. It was a gold captain's tunic from the original series.

"Better?" he said.

Leia ran her hands over his torso.

"It's a perfect fit," she said.

Jim glanced over at the door to the corner suite.

"Time to save the galaxy," he said.

"You won't have to do it all by yourself," Leia said. "You save us, and maybe we'll save you right back."

28

THE MENAGERIE, PART II

By the time Jim and Leia reemerged from Martock's room, it was nearly five o'clock. There was no time to waste.

The new uniform had the desired effect.

"Holy shit, captain on the bridge," Willy said.

"Listen up, everybody," Jim said. "We need to move in thirty minutes so I'll be quick. Ordinarily I'd plan an operation like this along military lines, but since you're all civilians I'll use a system you're more familiar with: Starfleet."

"Hold on," Gary interrupted. "How come you get to be captain? You said you didn't even like Star Trek."

"I never said I didn't like it," Jim reminded him. "I said I outgrew it. But if you're going to challenge my geek credentials, let's get it over with right now. Ask me anything you want."

"Anything?" Gary asked. "You do realize I've won every Star Trek trivia bowl I've ever participated in, right?"

"Anything," Jim repeated.

Gary mused for a moment. "The challenge will consist of three questions," he decided. "One easy, one medium, one hard. Are you ready?"

"We need to hurry," Jim reminded him.

"What musical instrument does Riker play?"

"The trombone."

"What was the name of the ship commanded by Picard before he took over the *Enterprise*?"

"The *Stargazer*."

"Final question: In what episode did Captain James T. Kirk first say the words, 'Beam me up, Scotty'?"

Jim wanted to laugh. He'd seen many a trivia bowl contestant go down in flames when confronted with this challenge. "That's a trick question," he said. "Kirk never actually said those words. Everyone thinks he did, but he didn't."

Gary seemed startled, but quickly raised his fingers in a crisp salute. "You are correct, Captain."

Jim looked around the room. "Does anyone else want to challenge my knowledge of this universe?"

His crew just stared back at him, awaiting orders.

"All right, then," he said. "Let me brief you on your mission. From this moment forward, I want you to consider yourself part of an away team on a hostile planet. Which isn't much of a stretch, considering the circumstances. Our job—our mission—is to get back to the ship and return to Federation space. Okay?"

Everyone nodded.

"I'm not blowing smoke about this. If things are as bad as they seem, it's important that we get out of here and report what's happened. Ensuring Dr. Sandoval's survival would be a coup all by itself. And we're the only ones who can do it."

"Because we're the only ship in the quadrant," Willy said.

"Exactly," Jim said. "I'll assume command for the full duration of this voyage. Leia is my Number One. If anything happens to me, she's in charge. Rayna is ship's counselor."

"And helmsman," his sister added.

"Counselor-slash-helmsman," Jim said. "Martock is chief of security. Dr. Sandoval is our science officer and chief medical officer."

"Dammit, Jim, he's an exobiologist, not an M.D.," Gary said.

"He'll do," Jim said. "Gary, I need you to be the extra set of eyes on everything—that means you're my yeoman."

"Yo, man!" Gary exclaimed, and then quickly offered a sheepish apology. "I never get tired of that joke."

"What about me?" Willy asked.

"You're our mascot," Jim said. "Our good-luck mascot."

"Can our mascot go by his real name?" Leia said. "Willy Makit is bad mojo."

"I don't want to," Willy said.

"No, she's right," Jim said. "We don't need to jinx ourselves. You need to lose the alias."

Willy's face turned as red as his shirt.

"You don't understand," he said. "My real name's Kenny."

Leia eyed Willy uncertainly.

"What's wrong with Kenny?" Leia asked. "Kenny what?"

"Dyes, ma'am. D-Y-E-S."

The kid produced his wallet and, with trembling fingers, extracted his driver's license. Leia leaned forward to inspect it. "Son of a gun," she said. "Kenny Dyes."

"Let's toss him out in the hallway," Gary said. "I'm not going anywhere with a walking, talking phaser target."

"Belay that shit," Jim said sharply. "We're all going on this mission. No one gets left behind. Willy is going to make it. Now before we leave, I need someone to pack up the minibars. Grab the candy and the nuts. Anything high-calorie and low-volume. We don't need to be weighed down." He looked over at Martock, who hadn't said a word since they arrived in Sandoval's suite. "Can you help with that?"

"Sorry," Martock replied, shaking his head. "But I'm not coming."

He stood up, walked over to the windows, and stared out at the city.

"Too bad," Gary said. "We could use that dude."

"No, we can't," Jim said. "We need the Klingon that's inside him."

Jim walked over to where Martock stood, listlessly looking at the dead city.

"So what's your plan?" he asked. "Wait for the bomb?"

"Sounds good to me," Martock said, not bothering to look at him.

"I can't let you do that."

"Really? Try and stop me."

Jim took a step back and set his feet firmly on the ground.

"Your dishonor makes you weak," he said.

There was a flash of real anger in the Klingon's eyes.

"Look, Jim, I don't know if you've gotten the memo yet, but we're screwed. If you want to go out there and die, go ahead. I'll stay behind and do it in here."

Jim raised his right hand and slapped Martock's face.

"Shut up," he said. "I don't need to hear your prattling. I know that the guy who owns a machine shop back in Atlanta is having a hard time handling this. I know he lost his friend. But I also think that, somewhere deep inside, Martock is still in there. And he wants vengeance."

The Klingon rubbed his cheek with a leather-swathed hand. He looked at Jim as if he were a particularly annoying insect.

"I'm done with this shit," he said.

"No, you're not!" Jim shouted back. "You're an expert weapons maker and second in command of the bird of prey Plank'Nar. Because that's what we need you to be right now. Do you understand? I need a Klingon who doesn't give a damn whether he lives or dies, as long as he kills plenty of zombies so he can brag about it to Karen in Sto'Vo'Kor. That's what she'd want, isn't it? For you to fight instead of quit?"

Jim stared at Martock.

Come on, you gigantic son of a bitch, buy into this, he thought. *I need you to get in the game.*

Martock stared back. Then, to Jim's immense relief, his mouth split into a pointy-toothed grin.

"You speak wisdom, human," he said. "Better to die a Klingon than live as a coward."

"Exactly," Jim said. "Now arm these poor civilians and get them ready for battle."

"My pleasure," Martock said. "It will be glorious."

He patted Jim on the shoulder.

"And if you slap me again, I'll kill you where you stand."

Jim grinned. "I would expect nothing less."

At five minutes to four, the team was as well-armed and well-prepared as it would ever be. Jim carried his trusty kar'takin and the Glock. He passed his Taser belt holster to Leia, who packed two extra Taser dart sets as well as her lirpa. Rayna carried the Mace clipped to her belt, plus a Taser. Gary and Willy got yans. Martock wielded his personal bat'leth. Sandoval got a Taser.

Time to go to red alert, Jim thought.

He looked through the door's peephole at the hallway. From there, he could see the entry to the west fire stairwell, just a few yards away. There were no zombies to impede their progress. It would be a quick thirty-second jump.

"Listen up," Jim said. "We're heading out in three minutes. Once I open this door, I don't want any talking. If you need to say something, whisper. I know we have weapons, but the zombies have numbers. We're not looking for a battle. Understand?"

His crewmembers nodded. Jim looked at their faces. There were so many other things he wanted them to know. But there wasn't time.

"We'll go in this order: myself and Leia, followed by Rayna and Gary. Then Martock, Sandoval, and Willy. Don't get separated. Stay with your apocalypse buddies at all times. Got it?"

Everyone nodded again. Jim could feel the tension rising.

"Keep moving. Don't give them time to gang up on you. Any questions?"

"What about Matt?" Gary said. "What if we run into him?"

Jim patted his Glock.

"I hope we do," he said. "But I doubt we'll be that lucky. I'm guessing he's being processed inside a zombie's GI tract about now."

Sandoval looked at his watch.

"We really should be going," he said. "After we reach our vehicle, we still have to drive far enough to reach minimum safe distance before the blast."

"You heard the man," Jim said. "Prepare for transport."

CHAPTER

29

THE ADVERSARY

Matt sat in a second-floor suite, calmly observing the zombies milling around just beneath his window. They slowly paced the atrium, spaced precisely three yards apart. Even as they lurched in seemingly random directions, they always maintained the same spacing. It was the perfect way, Matt realized, to blanket the entire area, to make sure no living thing passed undetected among them. They moved with the same mathematical precision displayed by flocking birds and schooling fish. The network was gloriously sophisticated in its design.

He leaned against the window frame with his left hand. His right hand—his *new* right hand—rested on his hip.

It had been a gift from his new benefactors. Matt didn't use the word *infection* to describe what happened. That term was too base for such a miracle.

Union seemed more appropriate.

He welcomed the visitors aboard, and in return they made him strong. And smarter. And they gave him a new hand. Or, rather, something better.

Matt 2.0, he thought as he raised his arm to admire its new shape.

At the end of his wrist sprouted a wild confusion of tentacles. At first they'd seemed to have minds of their own, writhing around with-out any input from him. But he soon asserted his mastery. They could pick things up. They could wrap themselves into a rock-hard knot for fighting. They could whip out as far as three feet in any direction.

He received this boon shortly after escaping from Jim and his own treasonous crew. He'd retreated to the second floor and broken into a suite situated directly beneath his old one. He evicted a couple of zombies to obtain it, tossing them into the hallway before slam-ming the door in their blood-caked faces.

Once inside he'd inspected the stump. There was no pain and precious little bleeding. This was puzzling, because it was a very seri-ous injury. The old Matt—the person he'd been just a few hours ago—would have fainted from the trauma. Maybe even died of blood loss.

But the new Matt didn't. Instead, he matter-of-factly located the room's microwave oven. He used his remaining hand to punch out the radiation-proof window on its door. Then he placed several glasses of water inside to keep the machine from arcing, clicked the door shut, and set it to run for an hour on maximum. Lastly he pulled up a chair and sat down no more than a foot from the humming device.

It occurred to him that he was getting quite a bit of microwave exposure. Probably more than was healthy for a human.

But then he remembered that human frailties weren't his prob-lem anymore.

The oven shut off five minutes before the hotel's power failed. Matt couldn't say for sure, but he felt that the microwaves had done him good—or, more accurately—done his new friends good.

He didn't realize how much until he raised his right arm and saw what had sprouted there. It was his reward for helping them.

It was also a first step, he somehow knew, down a road to even bigger changes.

The prospect didn't faze him. Emotions, human ones at least, didn't have much power over him anymore. Only the strongest stimuli—like the thought of killing Jim—roused them. That, and wreaking vengeance on the bitch who took his original hand. Fantasizing about what he might inflict on *her* produced a Technicolor grab bag of fantasies, all of them in bright crimson hues.

Suddenly, Matt felt an urge tickling up from the back of his mind. He couldn't quite grasp its subtleties, but he understood the overall meaning. He needed to go. The creatures sharing his mind felt it was time to move on. There was danger growing on the horizon. Matt needed to get to a safe place.

And he knew just how to get there.

His starship was waiting in the garage.

CHAPTER

APOCALYPSE RISING

The stairwell was illuminated by emergency lights at each land-ing and switchback. The mission got off to an easy start. There were no zombies on the sixth-floor landing or the fifth.

"Maybe we can skate right down to the basement," Rayna said.

A moment later, a single moan drifted up the stairs.

"I order you to quit saying optimistic things," Jim scolded. "Every time you do, something bad happens."

"Acknowledged," Rayna said.

Jim descended the stairs until the fourth-floor landing came into view, then stopped. He found a single ghoul pacing back and forth.

"I'll take care of this," he whispered.

"No," Gary said. "Let me do it. I need the practice."

Jim thought about the request. He had a point.

"Fine," he said. "Martock, will you back him up?"

"It would be my honor," the Klingon said.

"I don't need any help," Gary said.

"Martock's your second, like in a duel," Jim said. "He can give you advice. Now, do the deed."

Gary and Martock descended the stairs, making no attempt at stealth.

The zombie lurched toward Gary, its alien eye bulging out of its forehead. Gary raised his yan and swung it as hard as he could at the flesh-eater's neck. The blade struck spine and lodged there. Gary, panicking, tried to pull it out. But the zombie came with it.

"This blade sucks!" Gary exclaimed. "How the hell are you supposed to kill with this thing?"

Martock stepped forward, calmly took the hilt of the weapon, and then kicked the zombie in the middle of the chest. The blade wrenched free and the creature fell sprawling to the floor.

"Use more wrist in your attacks," Martock said, demonstrating with a quick gesture. "It will increase the power of your strike."

He returned the weapon to Gary as the zombie clambered to its feet and once more advanced. Its head listed to one side, the inner mechanics of its throat exposed by Gary's first blow. Gary dropped into a fighting stance and swung again. This time the yan cut cleanly, sending the head flying across the room.

A smattering of muted applause issued from the onlookers on the steps. Gary turned to them and bowed.

"Don't get cocky," Leia said. "There's plenty more where that one came from."

On the very next level they found three others. In the interests of expediency, Jim killed two while Leia broke in her lirpa, removing the top third of a hotel housekeeper's skull with one precise jab.

After the kill, she spotted Gary taking pictures of her with his cell phone.

"For Facebook," he explained.

Sandoval glanced at his watch. It was already a quarter after five.

"This is taking too long," he said. "We need to make up some time."

Just then a moan wafted up the stairwell. Followed by another. And another.

The group crept down until the second-floor landing came into view.

"Shit," Martock said.

"This is definitely not my fault," Rayna said. "I didn't make a single positive comment."

Jim stared downward, momentarily at a loss. It was his nightmare come true. The landing held perhaps fifteen zombies, packed together like commuters on a train. And the door to the landing stood open—blocked by a legless, limbless, well-chewed torso. Wearing a Wesley Crusher sweater.

Gary groaned quietly. "Not *now*, Wesley."

Jim's mind raced. The best approach would be to stand at the bottom of the stairs and kill them as they advanced. But an open door meant an endless supply of newcomers. Which meant wiping out every zombie on the floor. They'd finish up just in time to get nuked.

"Martock, Leia, and Gary, go to the bottom of the stairs and get their attention," Jim said. "Stand on the last couple of steps and take them out as they approach."

The three descended to within two steps of the floor and formed a line. The zombies reacted with a chorus of moans. Jim waited until they shambled clear of the door.

He looked over the rail at the next flight of stairs below. It was maybe a twelve-foot drop. A good landing was critical. He couldn't afford a twisted or broken ankle.

"What are you planning?" Rayna asked, eyeing her brother nervously.

"Something really stupid."

Then he climbed onto the rail and used it to launch himself down to the stairs below. By a miracle of balance, he managed to plant both feet cleanly on the same step. But then he almost toppled over backward. Only several embarrassing seconds of twists and arm waves saved him from disaster.

His balance recovered, Jim raced up the stairs to the landing. He used his kar'takin to take the heads of two zombies at the back of the crowd pressing in on the stairs.

Then he rushed to the stairway entrance, dragged Wesley Crusher clear with the blade of his weapon and shoved the door shut. This left half a dozen zombies in the stairwell, but they were easily outmatched by Leia, Martock, and Gary. Jim shouldered his blade and watched them finish. The last creature standing was a tall, thin man in a *Next Gen* uniform, vainly trying to climb over the bodies of his comrades.

Martock, impatient, descended to the lowest step and brought his bat'leth down in a high arc on the last survivor's skull. Its point struck home and the zombie went limp.

"Kapla!" the Klingon roared, raising his weapon over his head.

He didn't notice that one of the zombies in the pile wasn't dead at all. Just immobilized by the mass of corpses heaped on top of it. As Martock celebrated, it pushed itself free, grabbed his right leg, and sank its teeth into his boot.

"Khest'n!" Martock screamed as he fell backward.

He kicked the zombie in the face, breaking its grip. Gary brought his yan down on the monster's head.

Jim saw it all unfold. He ran to the stairs and dragged bodies out of the way, opening a corridor.

"Did the teeth get through?" he asked.

Martock pulled off his boot and examined his skin. So did Leia and Sandoval.

"It's okay," he said. "It didn't make it through the leather."

Leia nodded in agreement.

Martock started laughing.

"We have to keep moving," Jim said. "We're running out of time."

Martock put his boot back on and fell into line. The group trudged down to the first-floor landing. It was empty. Then they descended to the garage level. It was darker, grimier, and smelled of diesel, but it was zombie-free.

"End of the line," Jim said as he approached the door. "Good job, everybody."

It was a miracle, he thought. They'd made it this far without casualties or determined resistance. Things were looking up. Or looking up as much as they ever did in a place where the dead ruled.

He cracked open the door to the garage. Leia and Rayna joined him.

"What do you see?" they asked.

Oh, God, Jim thought.

He closed the door. Then he sat down on the floor.

"What's out there?" Leia asked.

"Borg," Jim said. "A whole bunch of gray-skinned, costume-wearing Borg."

"How many?" Rayna asked.

"I'd say it's the entire collective."

He glanced at his watch. Dawn was less than an hour away.

"And we've only got five minutes to fight our way through all of them."

CHAPTER

31

TO THE DEATH

Leia, Rayna, and the others took turns peeking out the door. They saw a sea of zombies dressed as Borg, all listlessly wandering among the cars, trucks, and buses. In the distance sat the USS *Stockard*.

"Am I crazy," Willy asked, "or is one of them carrying a trombone?"

"They're musicians," Martock replied. "They're on the schedule."

"What schedule?"

"The GulfCon schedule. They're an all-brass musical group called Seventy-Six Trom-Borgs."

"There's seventy-six of them?" Jim said.

"It's actually more than a hundred," Martock said. "Someone on their tour bus must have been infected. They never made it out of here."

"We can't let them delay us," Sandoval said.

"Here's how we'll play it," Jim replied. "You guys go for the RV. Martock and Gary and Leia, you stick close to Rayna. She's got the keys and she knows how to drive that thing. Sandoval and Willy, keep up. Get there, get aboard, and get out. Understand?"

"What about you?" Leia asked.

"I'm going to draw them off."

"Like hell you are," Rayna said.

"This level has a charging station for hotel golf carts. My friend Dexter used them for making the rounds at night. To check parking permits on all the vehicles." Jim explained that his plan was to commandeer a golf cart and drive to the far end of the parking garage—while hopefully diverting the Borg in the process. "Once you have a clear path, go to the RV. Then I'll drive over and join you."

"Bullshit," Leia said.

"It's our only chance."

"Then I'm going with you," Leia replied.

"I need you to stay with my sister. Later, if you still want to go joyriding in a golf cart, I'll see what we can do."

"It's decided," Sandoval said. "But we have to hurry."

Jim kissed Leia on the cheek.

"If you get killed, I'll never speak to you again," she said.

"Understood," Jim said. "Wait until they move off, then go."

He opened the door and stepped outside. The closest zombie spotted him instantly and moaned, alerting the rest. Jim added to their excitement by jumping up and down and waving his arms.

"Come on, you cybernetic assholes!" he shouted. "I've got something for you to assimilate right here!"

The words echoed off the garage's cement walls. The zombie Borg quickly obliged, shuffling after him as fast as their necrotic limbs allowed.

Jim trotted away to his left, toward the rows of trucks and cars. He planned to play a game of lifesize *Pac-Man* with the undead.

A Borg stepped out from behind a Chevy Tahoe. Jim split its head open with the kar'takin. He ran past another as he sprinted deeper into the car rows. He paused just long enough to gouge out its third eye.

"Wait!" he heard a shrill voice yell.

Jim turned to see Willy pursuing him.

"What are you doing?" he asked. "Why aren't you with the others?"

"I figured you could use some help. I call shotgun on the golf cart."

"There is no golf cart," Jim said. "I made it all up."

Willy was puzzled. "Then how are you going to get back to the RV?"

"I'm not going back to the RV," Jim explained, and he held up the Glock. "I'm going to lure them into a corner and then I'm going to use this on myself."

"A suicide mission?" Willy said, his face falling. "It figures."

They were interrupted by loud, continuous moaning. The Borg were coming. They surged among the cars like a tide.

"Let's not make this easy for them," Jim said. "You go that way and I'll go this way."

"Nice knowing you," Willy said.

"You, too, kid. Maybe Martock will write a Klingon battle song about us."

The Borg were within twenty feet when they split up and vanished down different rows.

Jim bobbed and weaved in and out of the parking lanes, making the chase as tough as possible for his clumsy pursuers. He was so successful, and led them so far astray, that he began to wonder if maybe, just maybe, he *could* double back to the *Stockard*.

Then he rounded a corner and came face-to-face with more than a dozen zombies.

He took off the first one's head. Then the second. But there were too many. For every one he destroyed, two or three more appeared.

Jim fell back among the cars. A zombie blocked his retreat. He sliced it open. Another one took its place. He was trapped between a service van and a big contractor-style pickup. He climbed into the truck's bed and then jumped on top of the cab. For the moment he was safe. Safe but surrounded.

He tried to catch a glimpse of the RV, but a bus blocked his view.

Soon the Borg were four ranks deep around the pickup. Their sheer mass shifted it back and forth. Jim struggled to keep his footing.

The arms of the closest zombies flailed across the roof, trying to catch his feet. Jim considered using the kar'takin but feared that swinging it would cause him to lose his already uncertain footing.

It's over, he thought.

He remembered the Glock in his belt. It was almost time to use it.

He wondered if Willy had fared any better.

Jim took out the pistol. He was about to cock it when he heard the squeal of tires. Then he saw, to his immense relief, that Willy had indeed fared better. Much, much better.

A black Hummer H2 was veering toward him with the high beams on, and Willy was behind the wheel, blasting the horn. The zombies recoiled from the pickup truck, agitated by the blinding lights. Jim leaped from the truck onto the hood of the Hummer, then scrambled up onto its roof. There was no time to get inside. He simply grabbed onto the overhead bars.

"Where the hell did you find this thing?" Jim shouted.

"Valet parking," Willy shouted back. "I thought about the Maserati but this seemed—"

"Just go!" Jim yelled. "Go, go, *go!*"

Willy pulled away in a screech of tires. The Hummer broke through a line of Borg, grinding over the brass instruments and fallen bodies while leaving a trail of crimson tire tracks in its wake.

32

LET THAT BE THEIR FINAL BATTLEFIELD

Incredibly, Jim's diversion worked perfectly. Almost every Borg pursued him. Only a handful remained in sight when Leia, Rayna, Martock, Gary, and Sandoval emerged from the stairwell.

"We're going to make it," Gary said.

"Stay quiet and be ready to move," Leia said. "This isn't over yet."

The handful of remaining Borg spotted them and shambled their way. Martock took the first one's head with a single bat'leth stroke. Leia flattened the next with a lirpa jab.

A Borg clutching a French horn blocked their path.

"My turn," Gary said.

He dispatched the zombie with a slashing blow to the chest that neatly bisected its third eye.

The RV was fifty feet away. It seemed untouched and undamaged.

Rayna pulled the keys out of her pocket, then dropped them.

"Shit!" she said.

She doubled back and picked them up. When she did, she noticed that more Borg were following them. And even more were coming from the direction that Jim had taken.

"They're doubling back," she said to Leia. "Do you think that means—"

"Get to the goddamn RV," Leia said. "We'll drive around the parking lot to pick up Jim."

They ran the final few yards to the side of the *Stockard*. Sandoval, Gary, and Martock took defensive positions near the door. Rayna unlocked it and stuck her head inside.

The vehicle was dark and seemingly empty.

"Looks good," she said. "I think . . . "

Before Rayna could finish her sentence—before she could do anything—Matt leapt down from the RV's roof and landed in front of Leia. He appeared to be carrying a giant, red octopus.

The octopus grabbed Leia by the throat; the tentacles wrapping around her neck like bands of steel. Matt hoisted her off the ground, then tossed her away. She landed in a heap, cracking her head against the concrete floor.

"Sorry, Princess," he said, "but GulfCon is a Trek-only event."

From behind his back, Matt revealed his custom-made bat'leth.

"I found this beautiful weapon on the floor of a restroom," he said. "Better late than never, huh, Martock?"

Rayna raised her Taser and fired.

Matt deflected the darts with his blade. Gary used the moment to charge with his yan, but he wasn't fast enough; Matt parried the blow—then, with superhuman speed, he used his own weapon to slash his opponent from neck to hip.

"No!" screamed Rayna, as Gary collapsed, a look of profound surprise on his face.

"Game over, Horta," Matt said. "I'm afraid your name will not be posted on the leaderboard."

Rayna rushed to Gary's side, but there was nothing to be done. She put her hand over his eyelids, closing them. "Warp speed," she whispered.

Martock charged, his own bat'leth ready for action.

"You will taste my steel, *peta*Q!" he roared.

"Taste *this*," Matt said.

His bat'leth cleaved the air with superhuman speed. Yet somehow Martock blocked the blow.

"Impressive!" Matt said. "I've wanted to give this thing a real test."

He attacked again. Martock blocked and counterattacked. Matt deftly avoided the strike. He was faster and stronger, but Martock had greater reach and far more experience. It wasn't a fair fight, but it was a fight.

As the two exchanged blows, Rayna scrambled to Leia's side.

"Are you okay?" Rayna asked.

Leia flailed around, searching for her lirpa. "Martock needs help."

"You'll get yourself killed," Rayna said.

Sandoval joined them.

"More Borg are approaching," he said. "We need to board the vehicle *now*."

Rayna grabbed Leia's left arm and hoisted her to her feet. With Sandoval's help, she was able to direct Leia to the RV. They were at the door, still struggling to get Leia to cooperate, when the clang of clashing bat'leths ceased.

They looked just in time to see Matt decapitating the Klingon with a final triumphant swing of his blade. "Hey, don't forget your friend!" he called after them. He lifted Martock's head by its hair and whipped it in their direction; it missed them by inches before shattering the windshield of a VW Jetta.

"God *damn* it!" Leia shouted, her voice cracking.

"Get on board," Rayna pleaded. "He's coming."

"No," Leia said.

She snatched the can of Mace clipped to the belt on Rayna's costume.

Matt charged across the parking lot. "Don't leave yet, guys! The trivia bowl starts right after breakfast. With Gary out of the picture, it's anybody's game!"

He grabbed Rayna by the shoulder and spun her around. She knocked off his Ray-Bans and leapt aside. Leia stood up, grabbed Matt's gold commodore's uniform by the collar, thrust the Mace can in front of his eyes, and sprayed.

The scream he uttered was fair reward, she decided, for the left-handed punch that once more smashed her to the ground.

His screams kept coming. Matt turned in circles, rubbing his eyes.

"You little filthy *patagh*!" he wailed. "I'm going to—"

He never finished the sentence. Willy bore down on him in the H2, Jim still lying prone on top. The immense vehicle struck Matt at full speed, launching him into the air. His body smashed into the side of the *Stockard*.

Jim climbed off the top of the H2. He froze for the briefest fraction of a second when he saw Gary's and Martock's bodies on the ground—then he pointed at the approaching Borg.

"Take care of them," he told Willy. "I'll handle Octopussy."

"Affirmative," Willy said, shifting into reverse and backing up into another crowd of shambling undead. Meanwhile, Jim prepared to face Matt once and for all.

Carrying his kar'takin in his left hand and the Glock in his right, he walked toward the RV. Rayna and Sandoval crouched beside Leia. She was hurt but still fighting to rise.

Matt slowly struggled to his feet.

"Par-tay's over, jerk-off," Jim said.

He leveled the Glock at Matt and fired three rounds into his chest.

The impact slammed him once more against the RV. Jim waited for him to crumple to the ground.

Instead, he laughed.

"I'm starting to hate that gun," he said.

Matt raised his right arm, revealing his new hand in all its glory. The tentacles lashed out and snatched the pistol from Jim's grasp.

"I've risen a few power levels since we last met," he explained. "Bullets don't work anymore. I've developed a super-fast healing factor that puts Wolverine to shame."

Jim watched as the tentacled horror at the end of Matt's arm explored every inch of the Glock. Then it quickly and expertly disassembled it. The pieces clattered to the floor.

"You're infected," Jim said. "You're one of them."

Matt laughed.

"Believe me, what I've become is far, far more profound. Comparing me to the zombies is like comparing *Star Trek* to old black-and-white *Flash Gordon*."

Jim brought his kar'takin into a defensive position and prepared for action.

"So what are you?"

Matt extended his right arm in the direction of his own bat'leth, which had been wrenched away by the H2 collision. A tentacle darted out, grabbed it and drew it to him.

"Isn't it obvious? I'm a reboot. Think of the human race as a long-running TV franchise. It's very successful, but it's tired. So you revive it by bringing in new blood and starting over."

"And you're the new blood?"

"No, *they* are. The miracles inside me. They were born long ago, out in the gulfs of space. And they're everywhere, floating from star to star, looking for planets on which to take root. Now they've come to Earth. The zombies were their first crude attempt to adapt to our biosphere. They're a failure. But me—us—we're the improved version. The best of them combined with the best of me."

"You sound like a great team," Jim said. "A bloodthirsty, grotesque parasite—and a space alien."

"I wouldn't expect you to understand. You can't imagine the vistas that have opened to me. My symbiote and I are so much more than either of us could ever be alone."

"I can see that," Jim said, eyeing Matt's tentacles. "If it's so wonderful, why didn't they grow you a new human hand instead of . . . that?"

"Because I'm not human anymore. I'm on my way to becoming something better. The fear, the apprehension that a mundane human might feel over such a metamorphosis is gone. The symbiote took care of that."

"I see," Jim said. "So they're not just adding stuff. They're deleting things too."

"I wouldn't put it that crassly. The trade is more than fair."

"Whatever you say. At least they didn't give you one of those God-awful third eyes."

Matt grinned viciously and pointed his new hand at Jim. The tentacles opened like a flower, revealing a red-pupiled eye at their center.

"Look at me, Jim. Look at your commodore. Respect the chain of command."

Jim fought the urge to make eye contact. "You know," he said, "it's really fitting that you came as a commodore this weekend."

"Why's that?"

"Because all the commodores who ever tried to pull rank on Captain Kirk were total douche-bags."

Anger flickered across Matt's face. The distraction gave Leia, who had risen to her feet, time enough to retrieve her lirpa. She hurled it like a spear at Matt's head.

Her aim was true. But Matt sensed the danger at the last possible moment. He lashed out with his right arm. The tentacles snagged the weapon in midflight. For a moment he stood there, the limb fully extended.

It was the only opening Jim needed. He raised the kar'takin and slammed it with all his might through Matt's elbow, severing the alien limb, and the eye with it.

Matt fell instantly, as if whoever had been operating his game controller dropped it. *Yeah*, thought Jim, nudging the inert body with his blade to make sure it was dead. *You're better than the zombies. But you still needed that eye, didn't you?*

A twitch of movement registered in his peripheral vision; he turned to see Matt's severed tentacles scrambling across the floor of the parking garage like an octopus run amok. With a furious roar, Jim leapt to its side and started hacking. "That's for Gary," he shouted with the downswing, "and that's for Martock, and *that's* for T'Poc, you murderous piece of disgusting alien *shit!*"

He was still slicing the appendages into tiny, wriggling pieces when Willy pulled up in the H2. The hood was strewn with zombie guts and there appeared to be a trombone stuck in its grill.

"Nice work," Jim told him. "Now get in the RV. We've got to move."

"I'm staying with the truck," Willy said.

"Fine. You lead the way."

Jim hopped aboard the RV. Rayna was already up front with Leia and Sandoval. She stepped on the gas and the vehicle lurched forward. Willy was just ahead of them, mowing down the remaining Borg and clearing a route through the garage. He crashed through the attendant gate and then pushed the accelerator to the floor, rocketing up the driveway ramp that led to the street. If any zombies were loitering about on the sidewalk, he intended to plow straight through them.

Willy emerged from the garage to find the street littered with abandoned vehicles. He slammed on the brakes and spun the wheel sharply, but the speed was too much for the top-heavy vehicle. The Hummer toppled over, its momentum carrying it to the far side of the road in a shower of sparks.

Straight into the side of a propane truck.

The resulting explosion immolated every zombie within a hundred feet. Rayna shielded her eyes from the blinding light and threw the RV into reverse, backing away from the blast.

"You've got to be kidding me," Jim gasped.

"He didn't deserve it," Rayna said angrily. "It isn't fair."

"Fair and fate are two very different things," Leia said.

Willy's funeral pyre illuminated the *Stockard* as it changed course and sped away in the opposite direction. Once clear of the Botany Bay, the RV's crew found the streets of downtown Houston empty. Many of the skyscrapers had gone dark, along with most of the street lamps.

At Sandoval's direction, they avoided main highways, fearing that the largest ones would be barricaded. Instead they drove on side streets, speeding past stop signs, racing beneath meaningless traffic signals, and pummeling over the occasional zombie that wandered off the sidewalks.

The one thing they did not see were survivors. No humans heard the RV approaching. No humans fled from their hiding places to beg for a ride. No humans appeared to be left.

It wasn't until they were outside the loop formed by Interstate 610 that they dared to get back on the highway. As they headed west, away from the city, the buildings began to shrink and eventually disappeared altogether. Soon they were on a deserted four-laner lined with dusty fields and barbed-wire fences.

For forty minutes, they sped in silence across the vacant fringes of Houston, Texas—and then, just as the first tendrils of sunlight flared on the eastern horizon, they caught sight of the highway mile marker they'd been waiting for.

"We made it," Sandoval said. "We're clear. Let the Air Force bomb the city all they want—we're outside any reasonable blast radius."

"It's over," Jim said to Leia.

He tried to take her into his arms, but she pushed him away.

"It's never over," she said. "Don't you remember *Aliens*? Or *Terminator*? Whenever the main characters relax and the audience thinks it's time for the closing credits, something else happens. You should know that."

"Are you serious?" Jim asked.

Leia frowned, got up, and walked to the RV's bathroom. She went inside and shut the door.

"Leave her alone," Rayna said. "We've been through a lot. She's been really strong so far, but maybe it's catching up with her."

Maybe, Jim thought. *Or maybe now that the crisis has passed, she doesn't want me around anymore.*

Leia returned from the bathroom, walked back to the front of the RV, and sat down.

"You okay?" Rayna asked.

"No," Leia said.

She crossed her arms and stared out the windshield.

"You want to talk?" Jim said.

"That's pretty much the last thing I want to do. I'm pissed as hell right now, and I don't make great conversation when I'm mad."

"Then just sit there," Jim said. "Sort it out while we drive. Maybe you'll feel better by the time we reach civilization."

A single tear escaped Leia's right eye.

"I can't *go* to civilization," she said.

"What the hell are you talking about?"

He started to reach for her.

"Get back!" Leia screamed. "Don't touch me. Just stay the hell away."

"Why?"

"Because Matt grabbed me by the throat with those tentacles of his."

"So what?"

"So the damn things had suckers. And the suckers had hooks on them. And they cut me."

She pulled back the collar of her costume to reveal a row of circular wounds on her neck. They were barely more than scratches.

But they were still bleeding.

"No," Jim said.

"Yes," Leia answered. "That son of a bitch killed me after all."

33

BLOOD FEVER

By the time the sun cleared the horizon, the *Stockard* was deep into West Texas, heading in the general direction of San Antonio. Rayna was still behind the wheel, with Jim standing next to her. Leia rode shotgun. As the miles rolled by she grew quieter and more despondent.

Sandoval sat at the table in the RV's kitchen area, picking at an apple.

Rayna glanced over at her cell phone, which sat on the dash. She picked it up and tried it, as she'd done approximately every five minutes since they started driving.

"I've got a signal!" she said.

"Call anyone, anywhere," Jim said.

Rayna dialed her college roommate and tried to explain in the context of a three-minute phone call that she'd just survived a zombie apocalypse. Judging from Rayna's speech patterns, Jim could tell that the roommate didn't believe a word of it.

"Rest of the country's fine," Rayna said after hanging up. "They're evacuating all of southeast Texas and the whole world is glued to CNN, but right now everyone's calling it a massive industrial accident. They've put up roadblocks across half the state. We should hit one before Columbus."

Leia winced with pain. Jim touched her shoulder. If there were roadblocks, there would be police officers. National Guard. They would be looking for infected civilians. The blood on Leia's neck would be a dead giveaway.

"Maybe we should park somewhere for a few minutes," Leia said. "Riding around in this thing is starting to get on my nerves."

"I'll look for someplace quiet," Rayna said.

"I can feel it happening," Leia told Jim.

"Keep fighting," Sandoval said. "Determined resistance inhibits the progress of the invaders. Unconscious specimens that can't fight back usually succumb in two or three hours. Conscious specimens can last much longer. The record, I believe, is fifteen hours, twenty-six minutes."

"Shut up," Leia said.

"Just offering my professional opinion."

"I need some alone time," Leia said.

"This thing has a bedroom," Rayna said.

"Perfect."

Leia rose and started toward the back of the RV. Then she stopped and turned.

"You coming?" she said to Jim.

"I thought you wanted . . ."

"Alone time. With you. Now come on."

Jim and Leia walked into Matt's bedroom and shut the door.

"Oh my God," Leia said as she surveyed her surroundings. "The dork side was strong in this one."

The decor in the RV's public areas was fairly ordinary. But in the bedroom Matt had given full reign to his fanboy fetish. A blanket emblazoned with the United Federation of Planets crest covered the bed. The pillows were adorned with threadbare Star Trek pillowcases. Above everything hung a richly framed oil portrait of Lieutenant Uhura, Nurse Christine Chapel, and Yeoman Janice Rand—all lounging on a four-post bed and completely nude.

"EBay sure is going to miss that guy," Jim said.

"A Hugh Hefner for the twenty-fourth century," Leia said, gesturing to a full bar stocked with bottles of Maker's Mark and Bacardi 151. She opened a humidor on the far end and showed Jim that it was full of cigars. "If I felt like celebrating, we could have one hell of a party."

Instead, she sat down on the corner of the bed, looked up at Jim, and patted the spot beside her.

"How are you feeling?" he asked as he sat down.

"Like I could fall asleep. But I won't because I know that's what they want. It would make things easier for them."

"I wish there was something I could do," Jim said.

"You're doing it now. Talk to me."

"We should have met sooner."

"Yes. But not that much sooner. I had way too many issues back in high school. All that crap with my parents. You wouldn't have been impressed."

"You should have seen *me*," Jim said. "One hundred sixty pounds, a raging case of acne, gold chains, baggy jeans, waving my hands and calling everybody 'dawg' . . . "

"A hip-hop hillbilly," Leia said.

"And an angry sci-fi nerd," he said. "We would have made one hell of a prom picture."

He put his arm around her waist.

"Thanks for sticking with me," Leia whispered.

"Of course I'm sticking with you," Jim said. "We're going to get you better. We've got Harvard's leading exobiologist onboard, and I'm much, much smarter than I look."

"Always thinking like a Trekkie," Leia said.

"Of course."

"But you know I'm going to die."

Jim winced at her language.

"I'm serious, Jim. I can feel them inside me, and I can't hold them back much longer. When Rayna finds a place to pull over . . . "

"No—"

"I'll get off the ship and I won't get back on. Do you understand?"

"Absolutely not. I won't leave you standing on the side of a highway."

"That's right," Leia said. "When you leave me, I don't want to be standing at all."

He grasped her meaning instantly.

"I can't do that," Jim said.

"You have to. I don't want to be one of those things, Jim. I'm really sorry you have to do it, but you're the captain. You don't have a choice."

"I've got to save you," he said.

"You already have. If it hadn't been for you, I'd still be in that hotel room, waiting to die. Or probably dead already. You spared me that. You gave me a few hours of hope. I'm not complaining."

Jim took her in his arms and tried to kiss her. She turned away.

"Don't," she said. "It's not worth the risk of infection."

Jim was about to disagree. About to say that kissing her would be the most worthwhile thing he could ever imagine. But just then he felt the RV make a leisurely turn, then slow to a halt. The engine shut off. A moment later they heard the door open and Rayna and Sandoval disembark.

"This is my stop," Leia said.

Suddenly a look of surprise and excruciating pain flashed across her face.

"What's wrong?" Jim asked.

"No . . . ," Leia groaned, pressing both hands to the sides of her head.

"Tell me—"

"The aliens. For just a minute I could . . . I could *hear* them. Not the ones inside me but . . . others."

"What are you talking about? We're miles from Houston."

She grimaced in agony. "We're miles from Houston but the . . . the network . . . it's followed us."

"That's not possible," Jim said. "This highway's been empty for miles. There's no one following us. And Matt's dead."

"Matt wasn't the only one," Leia said, her eyes growing wide. "There is . . . another."

34

THE BEST OF BOTH WORLDS

A few minutes later, Jim emerged from the RV. He carried the heavy flashlight from Leia's discarded gun belt in his right hand.

His sister had pulled into a seemingly empty rest stop. The *Stockard* was parked at the edge of its parking lot, near an area reserved for trucks and buses.

Sandoval sat at a weather-beaten picnic table under an oak tree. Rayna stood about fifty feet away, staring at the horizon.

Jim waved her over.

"Will you go talk to Leia?" he said. "I don't want her to be alone."

"Of course. What are you going to do?"

Jim tapped the flashlight gently against his leg.

"Wrap up some loose ends. I'll be back in a minute."

He walked over to the doctor and sat down opposite him at the picnic table.

"I can't help the woman," Sandoval said preemptively. "We've conducted hundreds of experiments. We've tried dozens of vaccines. There is no cure."

"I understand that," Jim said. "But how do you explain someone like Matt? He could speak, he could run, he had extraordinary strength. Why did the virus affect him differently?"

Sandoval shrugged. "If I had to hazard a guess, I'd say that he was a sort of carrier. The parasite that infected him had mutated in a way beneficial to its host. It kept him alive and healthy and sentient. It even augmented his cognitive, motor, and sensory functions. It really was a win–win situation."

"If you don't mind having an octopus for a hand."

"Well, yes. There's that."

"So, a certain fraction of those infected could turn out like Matt," Jim said. "Normal on the surface, yet teeming with parasites on the inside."

"Almost certainly," Sandoval said.

"That sounds like a very important discovery. Something our government should know right away. Why don't you call them?"

Jim produced his cell phone and placed it on the picnic table.

Sandoval stared at it.

"You know what I find strange?" Jim continued. "The fact that you're so relaxed. The zombie threat is still out there. Even a nuclear strike couldn't possibly get them all. But you're just eating apples and staring out the window. You haven't tried to call anyone since we left Houston. The world still needs saving, Doctor."

Sandoval kept looking at the phone. He made no attempt to pick it up.

"But perhaps," Jim said, "you aren't interested in saving it."

Sandoval seemed amused by the accusation.

"And here I was, hoping to win GulfCon's prize for most un-recognizable costume," he said. "How did you figure out my secret?"

"Leia did. She sensed that 'the network' was nearby." He gestured at the vast, empty landscape around them. "And since there's probably not much of a wireless connection in these parts, I figured it had to be you."

Sandoval leaned back from the table and crossed his arms.

"You figured correctly," he explained. "I was the very first person to have physical contact with the specimens. I was also the first infected. Not that I realized it. I developed flulike symptoms and went home early on a Friday. It was a holiday weekend, so I had three days to shake it off. Come Tuesday, I was back to my old self."

"Except that you weren't."

"Correct. I soon realized that I was no longer alone in my body. Naturally, I kept that information to myself. I continued studying the aliens, but with a new, radically different agenda."

"You weren't working to contain them," Jim said. "You were trying to help them."

Sandoval nodded.

"I learned, through my own experiments, that my blood was infectious. A single drop was enough to change other organisms. But only into simple zombies. The sort of symbiotic union I'd developed was exceedingly rare. I calculated that if everyone in the world was infected, only .6 percent of the victims would become like me. But that's still a significant number. Given a current world population of approximately seven billion, that works out to about forty-two million mutated individuals."

"A new species," Jim said.

"Correct. My benefactors were very interested in this prospect. They—we—formulated a way to make it happen. I hadn't planned to move this quickly, but events forced my hand. Last week several suspicious files were discovered and traced to me. An investigation was pending. I didn't want to be interred in a little steel box like the rest of the infectees. So I hacked into the facility's systems and disabled the security protocols. The complex was destroyed, hiding all traces of my activities. Then I neutralized the GulfCon attendees—a gathering, essentially, of all my greatest, most able adversaries. I infected the entire city of Houston with the pathogen, and the zombies did the rest."

"How did you spread the plague?" Jim asked.

"About a week ago, I purchased several dozen rats from pet stores, infected them with my blood, and released them in various high-traffic locations. Rodents are extremely effective disease transmitters. The affliction quickly jumped to the human population, then spread exponentially."

"You blamed Cronin, but he was just a victim, not the vector," Jim said. "No one person could spread a disease that quickly."

"True. If I'd had more time, I would have invented a better story for you and your friends. But I was thinking on my feet. Blaming Cronin seemed like something a group of laypeople might accept."

"Why didn't you help Matt? He was like you."

"Matt was a hybrid, but an imperfect one. The fusion process drove him insane. Still, my benefactors didn't want me to take a hand in his destruction. They left it to you."

"So who am I speaking to now? Your benefactors or Sandoval?"

"Truthfully, it's hard to tell anymore where they end and I begin."

"Where's your extra eye?"

Sandoval smiled.

"It's a little more involved than that," he said. "My benefactors have had years to make improvements. Have a look at what I mean."

He got up from the table, stepped back, and then pulled off his shirt.

At first Jim had trouble comprehending what he saw. Sandoval's chest seemed to be subdivided by what looked, at first glance, like an elaborate tattoo. Blood-red lines formed a complex geometric pattern that stretched from his neck to his waist. Four triangles ran up each side of his chest. Four large red rings sat just above his belt. Above those, a battery of smaller rings. And above that, centered on his ribcage, sat the biggest ring of all. It was about the size of a grapefruit.

"Watch," Sandoval said.

His torso began to move.

The triangles, Jim suddenly realized, weren't tattoos. They were skin flaps. The red lines were livid, blood-engorged flesh. As he watched, they slowly rose and fell.

"Auxiliary breathing apparatus," Sandoval said.

Tendrils and frills darted out of the smaller holes arrayed on his chest.

"Sensory organs," Sandoval offered.

Tentacles issued from the four holes just above his beltline.

"For manipulating objects," Sandoval said.

Finally, the big circle in the middle of his chest opened. It was an eye. The biggest alien eye Jim had yet seen.

"You're a monster," he said.

"You could say that. There's really not much of me left below the neck. They've done extensive remodeling."

Jim stood. The two circled each other slowly.

"I was planning my escape when you found me," Sandoval said. "Since your own mode of egress seemed sound, I tagged along. But now you and your friends have served your purpose. I'm truly sorry it has to end this way. But I must move on. The invasion isn't over. This is just a pause."

"That's where you're wrong," Jim said.

"Please don't get delusions of grandeur. I'm vastly stronger than Matt. One might even say invulnerable."

"No one's invulnerable. Especially against a person like me."
Sandoval smiled.

"Someone in a Star Trek uniform who thinks he's Captain Kirk?" he said.

"No. Someone who's entire world has blown up in his face. Someone who doesn't care if he dies, as long as he takes the thing that caused his pain with him."

Jim raised the flashlight. Sandoval looked at it with new interest. He noticed a white powder on the casing.

"You spend time in Afghanistan, you learn about IEDs," Jim said. "You learn how to spot them and how to make them. The RV had enough cleaning products and other chemicals to produce a really nice flashlight bomb. Anything I smack this against will be blown to bits. I can't wait to see what it does to you and your friends."

Jim leapt at Sandoval and swung the flashlight. The creature slid deftly out of the way.

He swung again. Another miss.

"Catch, you son of a bitch," Jim said.

He hurled the light straight at his opponent's chest.

With superhuman speed Sandoval caught it in his right hand and then tossed it away. It landed in the parking lot.

And didn't explode.

"A dud," Sandoval said as he turned to face Jim once more.

"No," Jim replied. "A diversion."

During the distraction, he'd reached behind his back and pulled out the two Tasers secured to his belt. He fired them simultaneously, at point-blank range, but Sandoval effortlessly sidestepped the darts. Then two of his tentacles lashed out and yanked the weapons from Jim's hands.

"Here's the irony of this situation," Sandoval said. "All this time, you've been trying to figure out a way to cure the woman. But the solution was literally in your hands. Electricity."

"I don't want to kill her."

Sandoval flung one of the Tasers across the parking lot. He adjusted the dial on the remaining weapon, upping the voltage to maximum.

"You wouldn't have had to," he explained as he worked. "In these early hours, the virus is very unstable. It's replicating within her body but it hasn't taken control of her neural system. You'll know it's reached maturity when the third eye appears. Until then it is sometimes possible to neutralize the virus with a high-voltage blast of current. Of course, it would have to be a pretty strong dose. Nearly enough to kill her."

He aimed the Taser at Jim's chest and grinned. "The only problem is that it hurts like a son of a bitch. Allow me to demonstrate."

For a moment, Jim didn't realize what had happened. Every muscle in his body seemed to cramp at once. He cried out through gritted teeth. His body, twitching from the voltage flowing through it, fell to the ground, landing him face-first in the dirt.

For the first few seconds, he was still capable of cognizant thought. He understood that the darts were delivering fifty thousand volts of electricity through his neuromuscular system. The only way to end the assault was to pull out the darts. But it was impossible. His body was no longer under his control.

He could see the USS *Stockard* across the parking lot, but there was no sign of Rayna or Leia. There would be no dramatic rescue. They had received their orders and were following them to the letter. Gradually, his consciousness began to dim, and then everything went black.

When Jim opened his eyes again, Sandoval was on the far end of the rest area, approaching the entrance of the RV. Jim's heart was racing, but otherwise he felt no lingering pain, no aches or cramps. He tried to push himself off the ground, but his muscles moved slowly, as if there were a three-second delay between his thoughts and his actions. It was as though his entire central nervous system had been reconfigured. The Taser lay discarded on the ground, just an arm's length away. Jim summoned just enough will to yank the darts out of his chest.

Across the rest area, Sandoval opened the door to the RV and climbed aboard. No doubt he was planning to kill Rayna and Leia, but of course Jim had anticipated that. Sandoval wouldn't find them waiting in the RV. The women had fled to the safety of the surrounding forest.

But now came the tricky part: Jim was counting on the fact that Sandoval would not pursue them, that he had nothing to gain by tracking them down. It was a risky assumption, but he had improvised the plan to the best of his ability. There wasn't much to work with, after all—just some expensive Cuban cigars, a bottle of Bacardi 151, and a threadbare Star Trek pillowcase.

The engine of the USS *Stockard* roared to life. The RV lurched forward as Sandoval cut a wide turn through the parking lot, turning the vehicle one hundred and eighty degrees. As the far side of the *Stockard* turned into view, Jim was relieved to see the bright orange flames were already rising out of its fuel tank. He covered his face with his hands just as the *Stockard* literally went airborne, propelled off the ground by an enormous explosion that sent flames billowing twenty feet high. Faux metal tubes and pieces of a fake satellite dish rained down from the sky. Clouds of gray smoke rolled across the parking lot, momentarily obscuring everything.

He pushed himself to his feet and tested his limbs. The three-second delay had vanished. He was whole again. He reached down to pick up the Taser.

When he looked up again, he saw his sister running toward him.

CHAPTER

35

ALL GOOD THINGS . . .

"Oh, my God," Rayna exclaimed. "Are you okay?"

"You did it," Jim said. "That was perfect. Where's Leia?"

Rayna pointed across the parking lot. "Sitting over there. She's getting really weak, Jim. She can't even walk—"

"Stay here," he said.

"What are you going to do?"

His sister looked like she was ten years old all over again. Jim didn't answer. He just started running. There was no way of knowing if Sandoval had told him the truth—but there was only one way to find out.

He found Leia sitting serenely at the base of an oak tree.

"That was an excellent plan, Captain," she said. "A double diversion. Kirk would be proud."

"It was half your idea," he reminded her. "Using the pillowcase as a fuse was an inspired touch."

"I was happy to be of service."

He knelt beside her, checking her neck and arms for any sign of an emerging third eye. For a moment, all seemed good—until his fingers found the boil on the back of her neck. It was a blotch of purple flesh about the size of a golf ball; the bruised skin pulsed beneath his touch.

"Is that what I think it is?" Leia asked.

"Don't give up yet," Jim told her. "There's a chance we can stop this thing."

He hastily explained what Sandoval had told him—that the parasites inside Leia might be extinguished until the moment the third eye emerged. He unzipped his duffel bag and loaded a fresh battery pack into the Taser. "If we hurry, it might work."

"How do we know he was telling the truth?" Leia asked.

"We don't," Jim said. "But we have to try."

Leia eyed Jim carefully.

"You don't need to lie to me," she said. "I'm not afraid to die."

"I've never lied to you about anything," Jim said. "I won't start now. But if this is going to work, it has to happen quickly."

She slowly, painfully stood up and turned her back to him, extending her arms. In just the span of a minute, the boil on the back of her neck had become darker and even more inflamed. It appeared to be twitching.

"Go ahead," Leia shouted. "What are you waiting for?"

"First, tell me your name," Jim said. "Your real name."

"I'll tell you if I survive."

"Tell me now," he said. "I have to know."

"It's Shelly."

"Shelly what?"

"Shelly Dumpkin."

"Seriously? Dumpkin?"

"I'll take your name when we get married," she promised him. "Assuming you can still handle the idea of a cross-genre relationship."

Jim didn't know if he could proceed. The pain of being tased was nothing compared to this. He was about to save the life of a woman he loved, or end it. He wanted more time. But every second of delay lengthened the odds.

A sudden flash of light drew his attention. Leia—*Shelly*, he thought—looked too. In the distance they saw an immense orange-red fireball broach the horizon and rise to the sky. It climbed and climbed, morphing into a towering mushroom cloud.

"Good-bye, Houston," he whispered.

"Hurry, Jim," she said. "It's happening."

Jim tore his eyes away from the conflagration and looked at her neck again. The boil was changing now. It appeared to be stretching, fluttering, boiling—

Hatching.

Jim pointed the Taser and fired.

The gun was at maximum setting. Though it took every last shard of his will, Jim kept the current flowing.

To make sure. One way or the other.

When it was over, Shelly's body lay still on the dusty Texas hard-pan.

Jim let the Taser fall from his hand.

I'll carry her all the way to the roadblock if I have to, he thought. *I won't leave her lying here in the middle of the woods. I'll bring her someplace safe. Where nothing can ever harm her again.*

He dropped to his knees beside her and stroked her hair.

The collar of Shelly's costume fell back, laying bare the wounds on her neck. Jim's vision was obscured by tears. It took him a few seconds to realize that the injuries had changed.

They weren't bleeding anymore.

Shelly stirred in his arms.

"I . . . ," she whispered.

Jim leaned closer. "You're all right? You can hear me?"

Shelly opened her eyes. "I . . . I felt . . . "

Jim lifted her by the shoulders, helping her sit up. "Take your time," he said. "Speak slowly. What are you trying to say?"

She coughed a few times, clearing her throat. "I felt a great disturbance in the force."

"What force?" he asked. "What are you talking about?"

"I'm quoting *Star Wars* dialogue," she said. "I do it whenever I'm nervous. I thought you'd figured that out by now."

"You're joking with me?" He wiped the tears from his face. "You're really okay?"

Shelly took stock of herself.

"I think so," she said. "I don't feel them anymore. And I don't feel sick."

Jim checked the marks on her neck once more.

"They aren't bleeding," he said. "I think it worked."

They embraced just as the shockwave from the nuclear blast arrived. Hot wind swept over their bodies, and the ground trembled under their feet. They barely noticed.

Rayna ran over to them. She'd wiped away her blue Andorian makeup and removed the antennae.

She saw the mushroom cloud and stopped.

"I think GulfCon is officially over," Jim said.

"And not a minute too soon," Shelly added.

Rayna said nothing. Instead, she enfolded Shelly in a crushing embrace.

"You're okay?" she asked, fresh tears streaming down her face.

"I think so," Shelly said. "I think we're all okay."

"Then we did it," Rayna exclaimed. "We're not in a zombie movie anymore. Or a video game. It's like we're back in a *Star Trek* episode, where we belong."

"Or maybe we're not in anything," Jim said. "Maybe this is a new story: Once upon a time, there were three people stranded in the middle of a desert. They had no vehicles, no plans, and no idea what to do next."

"I think they'd follow the highway to the next town," Shelly said. "But first they'd raid the rest area vending machines."

"That's right," Rayna said. "They'd grab all the food and drink they could carry. High-energy, low-volume stuff, like peanuts and candy bars."

Shelly nodded. "And they'd carry Tasers, in case there's trouble."

"A survival story," Rayna said.

"*Our* story," Jim said, turning to face the road. "And it starts right now."

*   *   *